OUT OF THE
DARKNESS

BOOK FIVE OF THE LIGHT SERIES

JACQUELINE BROWN

Cover art designed by Aero Gallerie

Also by Jacqueline Brown
The Light, Book One of The Light Series
Through the Ashes, Book Two of The Light Series
From the Shadows, Book Three of The Light Series
Into the Embers, Book Four of The Light Series
"Before the Silence," a Light Series Short Story
Awakening

To receive your FREE copy of *Before the Silence*, please
join the mailing list or visit www.Jacqueline-Brown.com

This work is dedicated to you, the readers, who have been as much a part of this journey as my characters. Thank you for your encouragement, excitement, and prayers.

Prologue

Washington, DC
The week before Thanksgiving, one year ago

He picked up his phone, anger seething through him. There was nothing unusual about this; anger was a cancer growing inside him, overpowering all other emotions. No one questioned his irate expressions or verbal rants. His employees were paid well, so they stayed. Those he socialized with were there for the money, power, and prestige he brought, not his personality. He had no one in his personal life except one daughter, who up until this moment had never challenged him.

I asked you a question, answer it, he demanded of his daughter. This text followed up the one he'd sent three hours ago: *Have you placed the order for Thanksgiving?*

That simple question required a simple yes or no response. She was not a stupid girl, unlike so many other women and men he was surrounded by; she was completely capable of answering the question and doing so now, not three hours later.

She understood the rules. He had made those perfectly clear throughout her life. When he spoke, she answered.

1

When he called, she answered. When he texted, she answered. And she did so immediately, not in a few minutes or a few hours or when she felt like it.

A thought entered his mind: Perhaps something had happened to keep her from answering his text. At this thought he stood, going swiftly to his office door. He abhorred yelling, found it one of the basest forms of human behavior, and so he avoided this particular expression of anger. His assistant, a small woman with timid eyes, was accustomed to his rapid appearance at her desk, with his face red and voice agitated.

"Check my daughter's social media accounts. Tell me if she's alive."

"Yes, sir," she said, and opened the social media accounts she had created specifically for this reason. She felt a pang of guilt every time she snooped on his child this way, but it was her job, she told herself.

"Well?" he asked after a few seconds.

"She checked into a coffee shop near her apartment thirty minutes ago," the assistant said.

He dug his heel, causing a squeaking sound to emerge from the wood floor. He spun his body, returning to his office, and picked up his phone from the burled walnut desk that cost more than the house he had grown up in.

Coffee! You're ignoring me because you're drinking coffee!

He typed because he was afraid if he used the speech-to-text feature, he would end up yelling.

Thanks for making this easier than I thought it would be. I'm not sure where I'm going for Thanksgiving, but it won't be with you.

He read the words and stood, his body shaking, and fumbled to push the Call button.

It went straight to voicemail. "Hi, you've reached my phone. Leave a message and I'll call you back." His daughter's chipper voice only served to infuriate him more. He paced, dropping his phone to keep from snapping it as he had the other three this year. He hit his shin on his chair and reacted without thought, lifting the chair, throwing it across the room. It bounced and broke.

He stared at it, surprised and embarrassed for a moment, that he had actually thrown a chair. Snapping a cell phone was one thing, throwing a chair was something more. He would think about that later. For now he had his daughter to deal with.

How dare you! he texted.

She responded: *I'm 21. It's time to stop pretending that we want to spend time together.*

You ungrateful—but before he could finish his thought a text came through.

I appreciate all the financial support you've given me during my life, and I hope this support will continue until

3

my graduation in May. Regardless of your decision in that area, it's time for me to do what's best for me. It is time for me to be healthy.

None of that sounded like his cowardly daughter.

"Who else checked into that coffee shop with her?" he screamed, forgetting that he abhorred yelling.

Two seconds later, his assistant entered his office, only mildly fazed by the broken chair or his raised voice. "The young women she is always with."

"And who are they?" he said with clenched teeth, though even a father as uninvolved as he could have guessed.

"Sara and Blaise, sir," the assistant said before leaving the room.

He took his phone to the couch in his office, the one that cost more than his assistant's salary.

He steadied himself. He was not dealing with Bria, he was dealing with her friends who thought they were doing what was best for her. But they were merely children who had no idea what was best for anyone, including themselves.

I would like for you to rethink your decision, he typed as calmly as he could. *Sara and Blaise are welcome to come to our home for Thanksgiving and* …

"Is she still dating that boy?" he called to his assistant.

"Yes, sir. She posted a picture of herself and Trent this morning."

Trent may come too, if you like.

He sat the phone on the polished coffee table and rubbed his hands on his knees.

She wrote back: *The apartment we shared together has never been my home.*

He believed it was her this time, not her friends.

He expected a surge of anger but it didn't come. Another emotion did, one he was far less familiar with, or at least far less familiar with these last eighteen years. He leaned his head back and stared at the white ceiling. Blinking, he felt sadness. For the briefest of moments his wife entered his mind. He physically shook his head to remove her image. It was too late—the thought of her reminded him of who he had once been and who Bria had once been. He remembered the bright-eyed child who loved and laughed.

"She's nothing like that now," he said softly to himself.

How could she be happy? Her mother and brother are dead. He winced at the thought.

"She could still be loved," his soft voice countered.

This was the voice he used to speak in, he realized. The voice that was his many years ago, before his heart hardened and the darkness overtook him. No one in his life would recognize this voice coming from him, not even his daughter.

You've done the best you could do, you've given her everything, the angry voice in his mind spewed. This voice had dominated his life since his wife and his son died.

"No," his soft voice choked. "I haven't given her love." A single tear slipped from his right eye, the first tear to do so since they had arrived in this city.

He leaned his head forward, rubbing his fingers through his graying hair. He cleared his throat and picked up the phone, his hands no longer shaking.

I'm sorry, he typed, and then placed his phone on the coffee table and stared at it.

He did not pray, because Holt Ford had given that up long ago, but he hoped—something almost as foreign. He hoped it was not too late for his only living child to feel the love from him she deserved.

After several minutes he stood and went to the broken chair in the middle of the room. He lifted it, putting it back on its casters. It slumped, no longer able to support any amount of weight. He held his hand on the leather, feeling incredible sadness for the pain he'd caused this inanimate object.

His phone buzzed, and he practically ran to it.

It was a client. A client that should be locked up but wasn't because of him. Guilt swept over him. He wondered what was happening to him. Why, after all the years, were these emotions surfacing now? The memory of carrying Bria, sobbing and confused, away from the casket that held her mother and her baby brother clouded Holt's mind.

Esther had insisted their son be named after him. The memory of her lying beside him in bed, her belly so large, her hand against his unshaven face, replaced the memory of her funeral.

"His name is Holt," she insisted.

He smiled as her finger traced his lips. "I appreciate that, but seriously, there are better names and better men to name him after."

She forced herself to a sitting position. He did the same.

"There is no better man on this planet than you," she said emphatically.

He kissed her. "Honey, Quint is better and he lives next door. I'm sure the rest of the planet has some pretty great guys too."

"Quint is wonderful, but you are more wonderful and you are the father of my children. I want our son to have your name. Please," she said, softening her voice as she leaned against his chest.

So tired. The pregnancy made her so tired.

The pain of the memory too much to withstand, he stumbled to the couch as his body crumpled like the broken chair and, unable to stand upright or support his own weight, he slipped to the floor.

His phone buzzed again.

I hope you have a nice Thanksgiving.

At her kindness, the tears began to rock his body. Tears he'd held in for so long came with such force he gasped for breath. He could not quiet the sobs even if he would've tried, but he didn't try. He thought about all those in his office who would hear the mighty Holt Ford sobbing like a baby.

He wiped his eyes and nose on the monogrammed cuff of his tailored shirt and picked up his phone.

Thank you. I hope you have a good break too. Maybe when you get back you could come home ... he deleted that word and added, *to our apartment for a day or so.*

He stared at the phone, hoping it was not too late for them.

No, I'm not going to be the one to make an effort, not anymore.

He deserved nothing less, he told himself.

Then I'll come to you and we can have dinner.

Whatever, she answered.

"She doesn't believe me," he said to himself.

Why should she? his thoughts answered. You've never set foot in any of her apartments. You've never gone out of your way for her. If she fit into your life, you allowed her presence; if she didn't, you didn't.

I'll be there, he responded.

Whatever it takes ... I'll be there.

One
BRIA

I awoke, the pit in my stomach growing with every moment of increasing awareness.

Sometimes when you wake up you forget the truths of the night before, hoping the thoughts forcing themselves into your consciousness are from a dream. Sometimes you can even trick yourself for a few minutes into believing that the awful reality of your dreams was just a dream, with no truth behind it. That worked in the past, but not this time. This time the truth of my conversation with Jonah was only made more real in my dreams of dead bodies lying beside a crumpled train.

I turned my eyes, careful not to alter my breath or move my body. He was asleep. I was glad for that. I didn't want to talk to him, not yet. I stared at the ceiling, made of narrow logs, the gaps stuffed with moss. Jonah had gathered the moss and cut the logs. He had lovingly placed each one where it lay so we would not have to share our honeymoon and first months of marriage with everyone in the main house. He loved me—I was sure—but I didn't feel that love right now. He always thought of me, putting my needs above his own, but not now, not when it came to this decision. Maybe that was why the pit was growing in my stomach. It wasn't just his desire to leave this place, it was his not putting me first, and that hurt.

Could I blame him? His sister was out there, alone, fighting to save the world. Could I blame him for wanting to try to help her?

His family blamed him for her not being here. They tried not to, but they did. What would they think when we told them we were leaving? Would they think that was what we should have done all along? Do anything we could to make sure she was alive and safe? Or would they see it as a foolish decision, like I did?

An image of my father entered my mind. I scrunched my eyes closed, trying to keep the tears in. I didn't want to lie in bed crying beside my husband. That was not how marriage was supposed to be.

I rose from the bed as swiftly as I could and left our hut. I went to the stream on the other side of the spring house and watched the water disappear into the stone building that my ancestors had built to keep food cold. More tears came, but it didn't matter; my weeping could not be heard above the sound of the moving water.

The dry summer wind lifted the tips of my hair. I looked at the sky. The moon was full, the wisps of translucent clouds layering in front of it creating an eerily calm glow, hiding all but the brightest stars. I closed my eyes, my neck stretched upward. The scent of jasmine permeated the air. I inhaled deeply, allowing its sweet scent to fill my lungs. I opened my eyes and lowered my head. The jasmine reminded me so much of what I wanted to forget, but it was not right to forget.

Jonah had a point: We couldn't hide here in our honeymoon suite while others were risking their lives. Perhaps there was a time when I could've ignored the truth, but that time was past, that me no longer existed.

Twigs snapped behind me. I didn't turn. I recognized his walk.

How bizarre was my world that I could recognize the sound of the man I loved by the sound the twigs made as they cracked beneath his feet. He stopped beside me, his legs folding gracefully as his body reached the ground. Our shoulders and hips pressed lightly against each other.

"It's a beautiful night," he said, turning to face me.

I lifted my shoulders and neck. "Yes," I answered.

He straightened his arms behind him, leaning back, staring up toward the heavens. "Is that jasmine?" he asked, inhaling.

I nodded. "Every time I smell it, I think of the girl Haz and Mrs. Pryce loved."

"Me too," he said, moving his right arm so it rested against my back.

I allowed his strength to hold me as I released my body into his. I turned to face him. His beard had returned.

Neither of us liked it, but razors were scarce. He kept it trimmed with his hunting knife, but I wouldn't let him shave with a knife. The risk of infection from an accidental cut was too great.

"I think you're right," I said, my body leaning closer to his. "We need to go back."

"Why do you think that?" he asked, his voice thoughtful.

"Sitting here reminded me of the point of life."

"To know God, love God, and serve God?" he said with a sly half smile, already aware that was not what I meant.

"To live intentionally and strive to help others," I said, returning the sly expression.

He tilted his head forward, his lips brushing mine as he said, "That's basically the same thing."

I leaned toward him, pressing my lips to his, and then pulling back as he moved his body closer to mine.

"Is it?" I asked, amused.

"In a loosely defined sort of way," he said, straightening his back as I leaned against his chest.

The leaves twisting in the trees slightly muffled the gurgling of the water. The moonlight dancing off the water gave the appearance of thousands of tiny lights.

I raised my head from his chest. "How are we going to find her?" I asked. "We don't even know where to look."

Jonah cringed.

"What is it?" I asked.

"Will you please consider staying here?" he asked, pleading.

"Will you?" I said in return.

"I can't," he said, sounding beaten.

I turned, sitting up onto my knees so my eyes were even with his. "I go with you, no matter where that is."

He turned away. I used my fingers to gently turn his face to mine and kissed his lips. "It's what I want, Jonah. I want to find her. I want to know she's okay. We can't stay here in paradise while she risks her life."

He laughed. "It's funny to hear you call this paradise. Our little shack doesn't even have electricity or a bathroom."

"It's not a shack," I said, feigning offense. "It's a quaint rustic cottage nestled by a gently flowing stream. And bathrooms are overrated."

He lifted an eyebrow.

"Okay, they totally aren't. I seriously miss indoor plumbing, but the other stuff isn't so bad."

"You're so different," he said, pushing a strand of hair behind my left ear.

"That's what makes people so resilient. We can adapt to our environment," I said, kissing him.

"It's not that you've adapted to outhouses and candles, it's that you're so full of life while doing it."

I thought for a moment. "I guess marriage agrees with me," I said, sitting back onto my heels as he leaned forward, closing the distance between us.

"Never in my wildest dreams did I think I could ever love as much as I do right now," he said.

My fingertips caressed his right ear as I slid a long strand of his hair from his face. "It is amazing, isn't it?" I said.

His hand went to mine and pulled it to his lips. He kissed the palm of my hand. "Thank you for being my wife."

I sat back, wrapping my arms around him as I lay against his chest.

"Thank you for asking me to be your wife," I said, the beauty of the moment making me forget for an instant why we were both awake and sitting by the stream in the middle of the night.

I hesitated, not wanting to ruin the mood, but decided it was necessary. "I think we should start searching in the town. Even if she's not there, I'm sure Mrs. Pryce will know where to find her."

He sat taller, propping himself against his left arm, his right one wrapped around me. "She will know where East intended to go, but …."

"Who knows where she actually is," I said, completing his thought.

He was silent.

"I guess it's the same as when we were looking for Sara and Blaise's families," I said.

"Except it's not," he said, his voice heavy. "When we left here five months ago to find them, we had no idea what we were going into. We didn't know what to expect. Now we do."

"We're stronger and wiser," I said. "We won't walk straight into danger without realizing it."

"When we went into the city and …" he fell silent.

"And met Trent," I said, finishing his sentence. "It's okay to say his name. He no longer has any power over me."

"I'm glad," he said. "But the memory of him, of all he did … to you. It's not easy for me."

I bit my lip and buried my face in his chest.

"We never could have predicted he would be there," Jonah said, as if blaming himself.

"You're worried about what we can't predict," I said.

Jonah leaned closer to me. "We are wiser and stronger and can avoid some dangers, but we'll never be able to avoid all of them," he said with a mixture of fear and anger.

I was silent, watching the moonlight reflect into sparkles dancing across the stream.

"That's life," I said, as an owl hooted in the distance. "We can avoid some dangers—the most obvious—but we'll never be able to avoid all of them. Even staying here has risks."

He lifted his head toward the stars.

"Staying here has risks, breathing has risks, but leaving here,"—he lowered his head—"that is inviting danger to walk beside us."

"What's the alternative? We stay here and spend our lives wondering and worrying about East. She may never come home. If we don't go to her, we may never see her again. Are you all right with that?"

"No," he said emphatically.

"Me either," I said. "I could live the rest of my life here beside you, perfectly happy, but we can do more. And I guess I think that if we can do more, we should."

"Is that a statement or a question?" he asked.

He was right. It wasn't clear from my tone of voice.

"It's a statement," I said, "but it's a strange one for me to make. I'm not used to sacrificing my own comfort or wants for those of others."

"This is more than comfort," Jonah said. "You aren't just being asked to give up hot showers or a soft mattress."

I leaned in closer to him, saying nothing. He was right. This was about far more than comfort, but I was right too.

This was something we had to do, not because we wanted to, but because we needed to.

"When do we leave?" I asked.

He exhaled and lowered his head, the side of his face leaning against the top of my head. "As soon as possible because every day puts us closer to winter."

"Then we'll tell the others tomorrow," I said, with a forced determination.

Thoughts of JP and my dad tried to intrude into my mind, and I pushed them aside. They were not helpful thoughts.

"Yes," he said, his voice sounding as though he was apologizing.

Two
East

The fighting never stopped; even during the darkest points of night the guns fired, almost rhythmically. Most nights I could sleep through it, but tonight was a struggle. Probably because we were closer now, close enough to see faces when we used the binoculars. This was the reason we had moved so close to the fighting. Haz wanted to see those fighting, to see if he recognized any of them.

He did. A few on either side. He respected none of them, before or after the light of the EMP. Some gunmen were from the police department—"The worst the city has to offer," Haz remarked in frustration. The others were politicians. Mostly local, all corrupt. John recognized only one and that one he had little to no respect for.

As I watched the battling groups earlier in the day, I was struck by how similar their leaders seemed, at least through the stolen high-powered binoculars. I couldn't hear their words, but I could watch their actions, and none struck me as caring about anything more than power. Day turned to night and the binoculars became useless. I wondered if the followers sensed the greed for power in their leaders.

The only good news came in the realization that Trent's commander, who came to us at the town, was not in any real position of power—an awareness that brought me unease and joy in almost equal amounts. I was glad he held no power, but I couldn't escape the feeling that it was only because those who led him were even crueler than him.

I glanced beside me. John was snoring softly.

"I'm glad he's asleep," Haz whispered.

I nodded. I liked John and so did Haz. He was a good man to his core, but that goodness made him hyper focused on finding his daughter. I supposed I couldn't blame him, but any time we weren't moving locations, he was pacing, asking us repeatedly when we could leave DC.

If I thought for a second that he would survive the trip to North Carolina without Haz and me, I would tell him how to find her, but I didn't. It wasn't that he was inept. On the contrary. He was bright and had more common sense than most, which mattered more than being bright. But the world was dangerous and complicated in ways it wasn't before the light. And he didn't understand this world.

He had survived the last nine months by being a prisoner, not by learning how to stay alive. He needed us to make that journey with him, or at least that's what I told myself. Though deep inside I accepted that my desire to lead him to Juliette was not one hundred percent altruistic. I wanted to go home. I wanted to see my family and hold my daughter. I wanted to make sure they were all safe and there were no new threats. I worried about them. What if they needed me? I would never know and that truth was consuming me with fear.

I turned back to the window, swallowing the fear that threatened to suffocate me. The firing started again.

"Is it for show?" I asked to no one in particular, though it was only Haz and a few of the freedom fighters near me and I wouldn't have expected the fighters to respond.

"Yes," Haz answered, turning away from the window. "At least right now it is."

They were firing at each other, but their distance was too far to do any actual damage.

I rubbed my hand through my hair. From the corner of my eye I saw Harley move to stand in front of the window.

"How many times have we told him to stay out of the full view of the window," Haz said in frustration.

Haz and I weren't on watch, but in actuality we were never not on watch.

"How can we leave them?" I said to Haz, quiet enough so the fighters wouldn't hear us.

I wanted to go. I wanted to get to Raven Rock, share the information we had, and then go home. I wanted to protect those I loved, but I felt protective of the fighters too. They were kids, though not much younger than me. Age didn't matter; maturity mattered and they weren't mature. Yes, they had survived the foster care system, but because of that, they believed they were untouchable. A dangerous, pride-filled belief. It's true Haz and I would never understand all they had experienced, but when we tried to explain that no one was untouchable and everyone had something to learn, they didn't listen. It was this cocky adolescent behavior that was going to get them or someone else killed.

"They survived this long," Haz said, as if trying to convince us both.

"I've never understood when people say things like that. All that means is they haven't been killed yet. It offers no assurance that they won't be. Harley and Xander take way too many risks. And no one can tell Amber anything she doesn't already know," I said. "They're kids, and they're going to get someone killed."

"These aren't like your pampered middle-class kids," Haz said, glancing in the direction of Harley, who was no longer standing in front of the window. The faint outline of a weapon hidden beneath his baggy slave clothes was apparent.

"You mean, not like you and me?" I said.

Haz and I might not be those pampered kids anymore, but we were before life made us adults. This was one of the few things we had in common. Our parents loved us and never hurt us, and they did their best to protect us. Our childhoods were nothing like those of the freedom fighters.

He laughed. "Yeah, not like you and me, they've always taken care of themselves. It made them into the survivors they are today. Besides, we promised John. We've learned what we needed to learn. It's time for us to go to Raven Rock and then to your place."

My body tightened at the mention of home. I thought of Quinn. How much had she grown in the few months since I'd been gone? Had she learned to read or finally learned to say the "Our Father" without forgetting the line about forgiving others? I shook my head, shaking away her image.

"We'll take him there when our job is done," I said. "I'm telling you we can't leave these kids here by themselves. They let us in, they let us keep our weapons, and they've made a million more mistakes since then. If we'd been anyone else, they'd be dead."

"We've talked to them about that. We've shown them how to better secure their hideouts," Haz said.

"They didn't pay attention," I said in frustration, at the memory of Amber half listening to our advice.

"They heard more than you think they did. They're smart kids. They're not going to let pride or stubbornness get them killed. They'll do what we recommended when we leave, just not in front of us. Besides, we asked them to come and they said no. What else are we supposed to do?"

"Make them come."

"Make them come?" he said, raising an eyebrow.

I nodded. I didn't care what he thought. I couldn't leave them here to die.

He reached his palm to my forehead. I swiped his hand away. I hated people touching me, even Haz.

"Sorry. Just checking to see if you have a fever, 'cause you sound delirious."

I glared at him. "This is no time for jokes."

"No, it's not, so stop making one! No one has ever *made* those kids do anything. And you're talking about dragging them—what, at gunpoint?—out of a city where everyone else wants to kill us and them. How is that going to work? And if, by some miracle it did work, we get out of the city and then what? We force them to march their way to Raven Rock? How long we gonna force them? They're people, albeit young people, but they're still people. They get to decide where they go in life, the same as you and me."

"They aren't like you and me. We can keep ourselves alive."

"They're alive, right?" He blinked at me.

"Ugh," I growled.

"East."

His voice had softened and he slowly moved his hand to my arm. I watched his hand touch the sleeve of my shirt.

"I understand you want to save them, I really do," he said. "But you can't force someone to be saved. Trust me, I tried. I would lock up kids to keep them off the street and away from the people trying to hurt them or use them. Eventually, though, I'd have to let them go, and they'd run right back to the dangers I'd taken them from, except this time they also ran from me because I did exactly what all those on the streets told them a cop would do, lock them up. That's when I lost them. Those first kids that I locked up, they never got near me or any of the men and women I worked with again. I learned, and with the next kids I built trust. I never tried to help them by arresting them. Instead, I arrested those exploiting them. I kept them safe that way. Bad stuff still happened, but by getting the ones hurting them off the street instead of the kids, other kids were safer. And by building trust, they started to go to some of the safe places and programs I asked them to go to. It was a longer road, but way more effective."

"That's awesome," I said in my most sarcastic voice. "You saved kids. Congratulations. What about these kids? There's no jail to lock the bad guys up in and no programs to send them to. It's us, we're it."

He straightened his arms against his folded knees, and his dimples began to show.

"What?" I said.

"You care way more than I realized."

I turned away. "Whatever," I said, making my voice sound harder.

He leaned toward me. I felt my body tense with the closeness. I wanted to scoot away, to create space. Not because I didn't like him that close, but because I didn't like any man that close. It filled me with fear. His face moved toward mine. I wanted to turn away. I wanted to lower my eyes, but I didn't. I kept my body as still as a statue as his cheek moved close to mine, the longer strands of his thin beard brushing against my face. I held my breath. Had I ever been this close to someone I wasn't fighting?

"Caring is a good thing," he said, his words warm in my ear. "I promise I wouldn't leave these kids here if I thought they were in any more danger than the rest of us. They're smart, and we've taught them. They're going to be okay. We need to leave DC today, the earlier the better." He shifted subtly back so he could look into my eyes. "You don't need to hide who you are, not from me. I won't use it against you. I promise." He hesitated.

For a moment I thought he might try to kiss me. Did I want him to kiss me?

He leaned back and turned away. I exhaled, my body losing its rigid stance.

John was awake, his eyes on us. Most fighters were asleep, the others dozing or on watch. Haz was right. If we were leaving today, now was the time.

Three
BRIA

We dressed and ate without saying much. We would tell our family and friends this morning. There was no putting it off. The pain in my stomach grew as I thought of my father. He needed me so much.

"Are you ready?" Jonah asked, extending his hand to me.

I stood, trying to push the thought of my father from my mind. I held Jonah's hand, the dread growing with each step on the well-worn path that connected our home to the rest of our family.

"Our parents won't understand," I said, feeling defeated by the very thought of the imminent conversation.

Jonah was silent; he didn't disagree with me.

Halfway down the path I asked, "What about the others? What do you think they'll say?"

"I'm not sure," he answered. "Josh, Blaise, and Sara have everyone they love here. They would have no reason to go with us."

"Except that they love us," I said, my voice choking.

He squeezed my hand. "Yes, they do love us. And they love East, but hopefully they'll let us go alone. We need to make the argument that it will be better, easier if it's just the two of us. Two people are easier to hide and feed."

"Easier to kill too," I said. One person on watch, one person sleeping—that would never deter anyone from an attack.

"Let's not bring up that point," Jonah said, putting his arm around me.

Entering the yard was like entering another world. It was alive with the activities of people and animals. Sara, Richard, and Eli were in the barn working on the final stages of the windmill. They would put it up soon, long before Jonah and I returned. Once it was up, there was, in Sara's words, a sixty/forty chance that it would actually produce electricity. If it functioned, she would start work on the many electrical priorities, the first being a freezer. She had plenty of parts she could scavenge from my childhood home and plenty more we could get from Mick's house. Heath and Maria said his yard and house were full of broken things. The mention of his name sent shivers through my body, though Sara was captivated by the possibility of having a junkyard at her disposal.

Sage emerged from the side of the barn, her belly pushing subtly against her shirt. On her arm, she carried a basket made from strips of cloth and woven vines, undoubtedly filled with eggs. Beside her, Maria and Heath's kids ran from the garden carrying weeds. Their dog

Franklin ran beside them, pouncing and playing with his young masters. The children tossed the weeds over the fence to the hogs and shrieked in delight when the giant male hog devoured them, while the female patiently allowed their babies to nurse. Max beat his sister back to the garden and pulled several weeds before returning to the hogs. Isabelle ran after him, pulling weeds and throwing them to the hogs. This time the mother hog stood and, leaving the piglets behind, went to the fence and ate her share of the sweet greens Isabelle and Max threw into the pen. The kids, Franklin, and the hogs could go on like that for hours and it was good that they could. There were always plenty of weeds in the garden. And since weeding was made into a game, the children were far more likely to do it.

"Maria is a smart mom to tell them to feed the weeds to the hogs," Jonah said.

"She reminds me of Marjorie having the kids paint the houses with mud," I said.

"I never would've thought of either of those," Jonah said.

"I think you get smarter when you have kids," I suggested.

He laughed. "That's funny, I always thought my parents were wrong about everything."

"No, you didn't. You loved your parents. It was my dad who was wrong about everything, but that's because he really was."

Juliette sat near the cold fire pit, methodically cleaning guns. Not an arm's length away, Astrea guarded her, as always. Based on the size of her protruding belly, her puppies would be here in a few weeks at most.

As we approached, Astrea lifted her head and wagged her tail, which had the effect of her tail repeatedly lifting and hitting the dirt. Juliette placed the gun she was cleaning carefully at her side and picked up Pops's fiddle. It was never far from her, something we were all thankful for. Her music added more beauty to our lives than she would ever know. She began playing the song she played at our wedding. She did this often when she saw us walking together, and every time it transported me to a place of majesty and peace, filled with love and hope.

Pulling me to him, Jonah said, "I wonder if I'll ever get tired of hearing that."

"I know I won't," I said as I waved to her.

She smiled broadly at the closeness of our bodies.

Nearer to the house, JP and Quinn were huddled near the kitchen door.

"What are you doing?" I asked JP as we stopped near them.

When Juliette finished her song, she and Astrea came to stand beside us. Juliette had a rifle on her back and a fiddle in her hand. The combination fit her perfectly.

"Painting spears," Quinn said without looking up from her task.

"Painting spears?" Jonah said.

"Yes, so I can find them better in the woods," JP said. "Juliette and I are going to go hunting and—"

"I promised I would only shoot if he missed with the spear first," Juliette said.

"That way, I can get in some practice and we won't lose any meat," JP said.

"That's a great idea," I said.

"It was my idea," Quinn said.

"No, it wasn't," JP retorted.

"Yes, it was!" Quinn said, her voice louder.

Juliette spoke, her tone calm. "It was Quinn's idea to paint the arrows, and JP's idea to make them, and I suggested he go hunting with me to practice."

"They aren't arrows," JP said in an insistent tone. "They're spears, like Jonah uses."

Jonah winked at Juliette and picked up one of the unpainted spears/arrows. They were the size of arrows, but as he held it in his hand he said, "You're right, JP, these are far too heavy to be arrows. The point is sharp and strong. Nice work."

I asked, "What are you using to make the paint?"

"Flowers," Quinn answered. "Some work better than others."

I peered down. Their brushes were made of twigs frayed at the end and they were using rocks to grind flowers into paste, adding drops of water when needed. Their hands were painted as much as the wooden spears were. Astrea went to Quinn and sniffed the concoction of liquefied flower petals. Quinn rubbed her head against Astrea's shoulder, Quinn's way of petting her without setting her paintbrush and spear in the dirt.

Quinn was decorating hers with beautiful flowers. JP had mixed all the colors together so that it was a brown color, much the same color as the wood of the spear, which sort of defeated the purpose of painting them. Juliette opened her mouth to say something, probably to point this out, but then closed it.

She had become, in many ways, exactly what East had asked, a big sister to JP and Quinn, except she was more patient than East would've been. She was amused, not irritated, by the silly things they did. When they started fighting—which was frequently—she would do her best to get one away from the other. Oftentimes, by playing a favorite song or giving them a lesson on the fiddle. JP, in particular, was picking it up well and could even read the music Juliette wrote for him.

Quinn, on the other hand, could not yet read music but had been given a gift far greater. She, like Juliette, could hear music in a way none of the rest of us could. "Perfect pitch" was what Juliette called it, a rare ability to hear a sound and know what note it was.

"Tell me when you're done with the spears," Juliette said, "and we can go scouting." She and Astrea returned to the nearby fire pit. Juliette placed the fiddle carefully on the stump beside her and continued cleaning the guns.

"Are Mom and Dad inside?" Jonah asked his little brother and sister.

"Yes," JP said, not bothering to look up from the painting.

"Thanks," Jonah answered, taking my hand and leading me toward the kitchen door. My hand was sweating with my awareness of the conversation we were about to have.

He opened the kitchen door. My dad's face lit up at the sight of me, and my heart broke at the sight of him. I didn't want to tell him we were leaving.

Nonie and Charlotte sat at the table sipping tea, while Quint and my dad stood, chopping garden vegetables that would make up the majority of the stew we would eat for dinner.

Thanks to the garden and Felicia's knowledge of wild edibles, we had been able to switch to a more plant-based diet.

Dad limped toward us, kissing me on the cheek. "It's nice to see you," he said. "Can I make you some breakfast?"

"The kids had blackberry corn cakes," Charlotte said.

"I had some too," Nonie added. "They were wonderful."

"Maybe a little later," I said. My father was taking my hand in his.

"Your hand is so cold," I said.

"It's a chilly morning," Nonie said, placing her hands on her ceramic mug to warm them.

It wasn't chilly; it was August. Only right before dawn was it remotely cool and this was hours past then, with a bright sun burning and no clouds.

"The stone walls do hold in the chill," Quint said, as if reading my mind.

He was right; it was slightly cooler inside than it had been in the yard.

Behind us the door opened and Sage wiggled past us into the kitchen.

"We got six today," she said, setting the basket in front of Nonie.

Nonie placed her crooked fingers onto the eggs.

"We've got to get a rooster," she said, with the same concern she said it every morning as our egg supply dwindled. Her hens were already a year old when the light hit; now older, their laying was decreasing. We needed more hens and younger ones. We needed a rooster.

"Heath and I are going to try to trade for one," Quint said to Nonie. "Once the piglets are weaned. We'll use Fulton and Talin and ride toward town. We'll take some of the rabbit furs, just in case we have to sweeten the deal," he said, reassuring her it would be all right.

And it would be. We now had breeding hogs as well as rabbits. We had no shortage of meat and the garden was producing enough that we were able to can at least some of the hardier produce. We wouldn't have enough to last all winter, but with the corn and acorns and the items we were able to can, along with the meat, we should be able to escape the winter without eating too many bugs or any tree bark. This winter should be nothing like what we experienced last winter.

"Have Blaise and Josh got any closer to catching a turkey?" Jonah asked, with a certain edge to his voice.

Nonie sat back in her seat. If we had a breeding pair of turkeys, she would worry far less.

"They are out checking the traps right now," Charlotte said, sipping her tea. "They should be back within the hour."

"I suppose they'll get one eventually," Nonie said, sipping the tea, her voice calmer. "They did get the rabbits and the hogs."

"Yes," Sage said as she backed away from the table, going toward the door. "I'm sure we'll eventually have plenty of egg layers around here." She was always doing her best to help the rest of us not worry, something we all appreciated.

"If you don't want breakfast, can I get you some tea or water?" Dad asked, typical of the doting parent he now was.

"No," Jonah said, "we were actually coming to tell you all something."

They turned to us. A joyful expression spread across Nonie's face, causing the wrinkles around her eyes to deepen. "You're pregnant," she said, clapping her hands in happiness.

Charlotte stood in excitement. Sage turned, facing me, mouth open in surprise.

"No," Jonah said, with force. "No, we aren't."

Sage closed her mouth and slipped out the door. I didn't blame her; I wished I could leave this conversation.

Charlotte returned to her place at the table, Dad going to sit beside her. Both of them wore concerned expressions.

"What is it?" Quint asked, setting the knife he'd been using on the cutting board and wiping his hands on a kitchen towel.

"I," Jonah said,—I squeezed his hand—"we have decided to find East and bring her home if we can."

The room was silent as his words settled in the minds of our parents and grandmother. Charlotte's face was the first to register understanding. She blinked and promptly left the room. A moment later Nonie stood from her spot at the table and followed her. We were left with only Quint and my father. Neither of them was looking at us, both staring down. My father's hand rubbed the cane Quint had made for him.

Quint and my father made eye contact with one another.

"I better go check on them." Quint's words were directed to my dad, not to us. Quint pushed his body from the counter, his long legs taking him halfway across the kitchen in only a few steps.

My father came toward us. My body trembled at the hurt he must be feeling. He stood in front of me and opened his arms. I held him.

"I understand," he said, his voice strong. "You two must do what you believe the Lord is calling you to do."

I bit my lip. Is this what God was asking us to do or even wanted us to do? I had no idea.

"I can't leave East out there," Jonah said, as if apologizing to my father.

My dad stepped back, leaning heavily on the cane. "I never had a sister or brother, so I can't say that I understand that feeling, but I understand what it means to love," he said, the side of his body pressing against mine.

"Will you talk to them?" Jonah asked. "Help them understand?"

My father placed a hand on Jonah's shoulder. "Son, they understand. They're torn. They want you safe, but they want your sister home. Quint feels like a coward for not having already gone himself and searched for her."

Jonah cringed, no doubt at the memory of himself calling his dad a coward when once before he didn't protect East the way Jonah thought he should have.

"My father is the bravest man I know," Jonah said.

"Trust me," my dad said, "I've told him that a hundred times. Still, it's hard when your child's in danger, not to run after her. Even if it's a danger they chose to encounter."

"If he thinks he should go after her, then why hasn't he?" I asked, though I was glad he hadn't. His place was here. That was obvious to me and I'm sure to everyone else, but I wondered what kept him here.

"He wishes he could go to her, to protect her, and bring her home, but the Lord has said no, for reasons Quint doesn't fully understand. Though they are obvious to me.

His wife is here, his young children are here, his mother is here. This is where he is most needed. Thankfully, Quint is wise enough to listen to God and not his own desires."

"How does he know the difference between what he wants and what God wants?" I asked, never understanding when any of them spoke in this way about God.

"God will make it clear," my father—the former militant atheist who now found a way to bring God into every conversation—answered.

His answer brought me no clarity, only more confusion.

Breaking the quiet contemplation, Dad asked, "Have you told the others?"

I shook my head.

"When do you plan—to leave?" When his voice caught, I realized how devastated he was and how brave he was trying to be at this moment.

"A few days," Jonah said, lifting his head.

My father forced a smile. "You should go to your friends and tell them. Give them time to accept things before you leave." His voice cracked.

"We wanted to tell you first," I said.

My father sniffed and nodded. "Thank you for that," he said, with another forced smile. "I need to find Quint and Charlotte now." His expression fell as he turned from us. He leaned on his cane as he limped slowly from the kitchen. He did not turn back. The door swung shut behind him and only then did he allow the tears. We listened to his muffled sobs. I started toward the hallway door but fell into the chair, my tears coming too fast to see.

Jonah came to my side. He sat and wrapped his arm around me. I leaned against him and cried.

"Your dad needs you," he said. "Stay and watch over him. I'll be back before you even realize I'm gone."

I wiped my eyes. "Till death do us part," I said.

"That isn't meant to be taken literally. We can be physically apart."

"Don't you understand? When I said before I wasn't strong enough to keep the home fires burning, that wasn't just something to say to try to prove a point. It was the truth. Back before things changed, I used to look at those families torn apart by travel and be in awe of them, thinking I would never be strong enough to let the man I loved be so far away from me. Now that I have you, I know I was right. All the women and men before, who were in the military … their sacrifice was so great, but those who stayed behind and had to continue on without them, they were sacrificing more, and I can't sacrifice that much. I can't be away from you, not like that. I'm being childish, but it doesn't matter. Where you go, I go."

He held me. "I would be just as childish if the situation were reversed."

Four
BRIA

The sun warmed me, and I was grateful for the brightness it brought to this moment of sadness. The kids were playing like they had been before we went into the house. Franklin chased after Max and Isabelle. Astrea lay peacefully beside Juliette, who had finished cleaning the guns and now sat near JP and Quinn. The younger two were still painting as Juliette played the song she played most often, "The Sound of Silence." It no longer made me cry as it had that first night in the old church. In the months since then it had taken on a different tone. No longer was it a prayer of anguished sorrow sent to the heavens on the wings of music; it wafted gently above, still infused with sadness, yet now mixed with a degree of gratitude and acceptance.

Blaise asked Juliette, once, when it was just the two of them, who she played it for, for more than anything else it was clear it was played for someone. Blaise said at first she thought Juliette didn't hear her. She was silent for so long, but finally she softly whispered, "My dad." Blaise said she regretted asking Juliette because she hadn't spoken again for more than a day. The pain of that memory was too much, even almost nine months after losing him. Perhaps someday she would be able to tell us about her family and her previous life. If she did, it would be at a time when she chose to do so. None of us would ever ask her again, not because we weren't curious or didn't care, but because it was too painful to watch her agony.

Juliette and the younger children ignored us. The only other person in the yard was Eli, sitting on one of the numerous logs that surrounded the darkened fire pit, his prayer book in hand.

We went toward him. We would tell him first; it would be easier. He loved us and would miss us, but not like the others. He loved all of us deeply, but with an element of detachment. It was difficult to explain with words, though it could be sensed easily.

Jonah released my hand as he sat across from his brother. I sat beside Jonah and stared at Eli's feet. His black shoes were worn, covered with dirt. I wondered if they were ever dirty, before, when his days were spent in a church instead of a farm.

After a few moments, Eli closed his book and gradually lifted his gaze to his brother and then to me. "I hear you aren't pregnant," he said, winking.

"Sage told you?" Jonah asked.

He nodded. "She said you two were talking about something serious with the parents and that you weren't pregnant."

"Where is she?" I asked, scanning the yard.

"I think she's in Sara's workshop," Eli answered.

I turned in the direction of the barn. Her workshop occupied its far end, with the hogs occupying the front and the horses and chickens the middle.

"We told them we're leaving," Jonah answered.

"Leaving?" Eli said, raising an eyebrow.

"To search for East."

Eli straightened his legs, his shoes sliding in the dirt.

"Do you think you can find her?"

Jonah nodded. "We'll go to the town where we found Sage. She'll either be there or they'll know where to find her."

Eli leaned back, staring past us at the grass growing behind the dirt that surrounded the fire pit.

"I miss lawn mowers," he said pensively.

"Lawn mowers?" I said, sure I misheard. Sure he meant to say he missed his sister or he would miss us.

"Yeah, I miss lawn mowers. Stupid, right?" He pulled his legs to him and sat forward, somehow reminding me of JP.

"Kind of," I said.

He leaned forward, almost lying on his thighs, his hands looped over his neck and pulling his body toward the ground as he sat on the log. A moment later he sat upright as if forcing nervous energy from his body.

"Whenever life was confusing or unclear, I would mow the lawn and things would become less overwhelming. The order, the neatness, it was settling and gratifying. Life as a priest was neither orderly or neat. Most days I was all right with the chaos that comes with serving others, but some days I really needed to bring order to some small part of the world. Right now is one of those moments," Eli said, rubbing his hands vigorously on the outside of his thighs.

"What did you do in the winter?" Jonah asked, watching his brother.

Eli stopped rubbing his legs. "I'd shovel snow or if it wasn't too cold, pressure wash. I'm going with you," he said, abruptly standing, his body no longer able to contain the energy in the sitting position.

Jonah stood and I followed.

"They need you here," Jonah said, his voice calm yet determined.

Eli paced and shook his head. "I've known for a while I needed to go, but I've been afraid." He shook his head. "I admire the martyrs who died for their faith, and yet I've been too scared to leave my parents' home."

"Perhaps you were being wise and prudent." These were words I had learned from Sara, and she had learned them from him.

"I was being a coward," he responded. "You all went and my baby sister is still out there and I've stayed here."

"You were needed here, you are *still* needed here," Jonah said.

"What will they do here without the Eucharist?" I asked, knowing that for my father and Sara, life revolved around the tiny pieces of consecrated bread they received from Eli.

He stopped pacing and said, "I'll build a tabernacle and consecrate enough hosts to last while I'm gone."

"And how long will that be?" Jonah asked thoughtfully. "Our plan is to be back before winter, but the truth is we don't know when we'll be back or even if we will. Your leaving puts our family without a priest."

"And my staying puts DC without one," Eli countered.

"We don't know that there aren't other priests in DC," Jonah said.

"And we don't know that there are," Eli responded.

"Your parents will be devastated," I said, feeling the tears well on Charlotte's behalf.

"My parents are stronger than you think," Eli answered. "They understand their children have their own lives to live, their own sacrifices to make."

From across the yard I saw Sage and Sara, and an image of Faith, Sara's mom, came into my mind. "Yes, but it doesn't make them hurt less."

He put his hands in his pockets, reminding me of Jonah.

"It's what I have to do." He turned as he said the words and left the fire pit.

We watched him walk swiftly to the barn. His head down, he almost ran into Sage and Sara, who had now been joined by Blaise and Josh.

They watched him in silence, expressions of concern on their faces. When he disappeared into the barn, their attention shifted to us. They came toward us.

"We might as well sit," I said to Jonah. "This isn't going to be a short conversation."

It was only morning and already I felt fatigued. So much had changed in my life; however, the one constant was a desire to sleep when things became hard. Jonah sat beside me, and I stared at the ashes of last night's fire. The children must have asked for it after Jonah and I had gone to our home. While he was telling me he wanted to return to DC and my world was spinning, the others probably sat here listening to Juliette play the fiddle and listening to stories told by Nonie, about her days as a girl on her grandparents' farm—days very much like these.

Our friends stepped over the logs and sat around the circle. Sara chose a spot on a log beside me and Blaise plopped down onto the ground in front of me.

"What's going on?" Blaise said, her elbows leaning against her crossed legs, her chin supported by her folded hands, her eyes wide and curious, not at all fearful—so much like a trusting child, though she was far from this. Inside her calm exterior was the most cunning hunter among us.

She was someone I wished could come with us because it would make the journey easier in so many ways, and someone I prayed would be wise enough to stay here. I was silent.

Beside me, Jonah exhaled loudly and said, "We told our parents we're leaving soon, to find East."

The space was silent for many seconds, except for the sound of Juliette's hurried music in the distance. The franticness of the piece was not helping me stay calm.

"How will you find her?" Blaise asked quietly, the relaxed, inquisitive posture of her body unmoved.

"We'll start at the town and go from there," Jonah said. "She'll either be there or Mrs. Pryce will know where to find her."

"What if she doesn't?" Blaise asked.

"Or what if the town isn't there anymore?" Josh said, eyeing Blaise and trying to read the cryptic expression on her face.

"We found everyone else, we can find East," I said with forced confidence.

My friends were once again silent, lost in thought. Juliette's music had shifted. It was slower now, and sadder, though perhaps that was what I brought to it, rather than what it brought to me.

"What did your dad say?" Sara asked, her hand going to my leg.

Tears attacked me and I couldn't speak.

"He understands," Jonah said.

Sage asked, "And your parents and Nonie?"

"They will understand," Jonah responded. "We won't be gone long."

Josh laughed. "Famous last words if I ever heard 'em."

I expected Blaise to admonish Josh for his bluntness, but she remained silent, lost in thought.

"What did Eli say?" Sara asked, with an edge of apprehension.

Jonah ran his fingers through his hair in frustration. He didn't want Eli to come. It was bad enough I was risking my life; he didn't want to take another child from his parents.

"He wants to go," I said.

"There will be no priest here, no Eucharist," Sara said with concern.

"He said he'll build a tabernacle," Jonah said, "and consecrate as many hosts as he can."

Her body relaxed, though she tried not to let it show. "Why is he going?" she asked.

"He said he's known for a while it's what he needed to do," I said.

Sara stared at the ground, her expression torn. She didn't want to go, but she thought she should.

"Your place is here," I said, taking her hand in mine and squeezing it to get her attention. "And so is yours," I added preemptively to Blaise.

"You came with us to search for our families," Sara said.

"Yes, and now your families are here," I said.

"Sara's right. It's only fair that we come with you," Blaise said.

"We've done that before, where one of us goes and the rest follow," Jonah said, his voice commanding. "That's not going to happen this time. Our lives are here, all of our lives. Bria and I will go and bring East back, if we can. Eli said he's coming with us. He doesn't know what he's saying yes to. You do. Don't come. And do what you can to convince him to stay. It's bad enough Bria's coming."

He stood. I watched as he walked toward the barn. Josh moved to his spot beside me.

"We can't let you go without us," Sara said.

"You and Sage belong here," I said.

Sara sat back in silence. Sage belonged here and Sage would never stay if Sara left.

"I can go," Sage said with defiance.

"Of course you *can*," I said. "But you would be risking your life and your baby's."

Sara turned her attention to her sister. "I think we should sit this one out," Sara said, as if it was a game of kickball.

Sage's hand moved to her belly. "Pregnancy is not a disease," she said. "I can do just as much as anyone else."

"Of course it's not a disease, it's a gift," Blaise said. "And so far, it's been a gift with no complications. But that could change at any moment."

"I'm not worried," Sage said, false confidence hiding the doubt.

"You would be risking our lives if something happened to you and the baby," I said, trying to be kind and not harsh, though harsh is how I felt. It was foolish of her to risk so much unnecessarily.

Sara touched Sage's arm. "Bria and Blaise are right. It's been a really easy pregnancy so far, but that could change, and if it does, the mission is no longer about finding East, it's about keeping you and baby alive."

"I would never ask the mission to change," Sage said.

Josh leaned forward. "It doesn't matter, it just would. Accept it and move on, and by that I mean accept that you need to sit this one out. Blaise and I will be sure and take out some harvesters for you," he said, winking. His voice sounded overly confident, an act to hide the fear he felt.

"They need you two here," I said to Josh and Blaise, though selfishly I wanted them with me.

"Juliette and Quint can hunt just as good as us and Heath is strong and, as Sage says, she can do as much as anyone else," Blaise said.

"What about your parents?" I asked.

She shrugged. "They'll deal or they won't."

Her relationship with her parents had gotten better, but it was still far from what it was before the harvesters' camp.

"You're making a mistake. Remember how dangerous the world is now," I said.

"We survived before, we'll survive again," Josh said in his too confident voice.

"Nothing is guaranteed, Josh," Sara cautioned.

"Nothing can hurt me when I've got Blaise by my side," Josh said, holding his hand out for his wife. She took it. He pulled her up and in a moment she was sitting on his lap.

"What if something happens to her?" Sage asked softly.

"Nothing can hurt me as long as I've got Josh by my side," Blaise said, her arms around Josh's neck.

In my stomach the pit grew.

Five
EAST

The three of us made our way between buildings, avoiding those streets with the most gunfire. The constant popping in the distance was methodical and obnoxious—a waste of ammunition that did nothing to secure our nation or even our capital.

"That's a lot of gunfire for forces that aren't part of the government," John said from in front of me.

"It's not as much you might think," Haz said, edging his way out of a doorway.

"The firing never stops," John said in disagreement.

"It's slow and steady. They aren't burning through a ton of rounds at that speed. We had more than enough ammo in our police department alone, to supply one side for a few weeks, at the rate they're going," Haz said.

"You think they broke into the police department?" I asked.

"I know they did. I helped them," Haz said as we continued forward, moving beyond the fight. "In the beginning we needed law and order. The military—or what I thought was the military—stepped in to provide that. I did what I could to help them. That included getting them weapons and bullets from the police department storerooms. Once I realized what they were becoming, I regretted that decision. Still, I believed they were the government. Now I think they're no better than the rebels, maybe worse. At least the rebels don't claim to be something they aren't."

"It's not your fault," I said as I jogged behind him.

"I did what I thought was best," he acknowledged, "but that doesn't let me off the hook."

I believed as he did, but my parents had always told me I was too demanding of myself and others. I never agreed with them. At the end of the day, if evil results from our actions—no matter how well intentioned those actions—there is still evil in the world that wasn't there before. People telling you it wasn't your fault didn't change that.

Silently I hoped I'd never again see Derrick, the man we helped rescue, the man John and Pam said helped orchestrate the attack. I didn't believe in killing people unless it was to protect myself or someone else, but it would be difficult not to kill him. I forced my mind to shift, to keep thoughts of revenge from overtaking me.

Our goodbye to the freedom fighters was wholly unemotional; the fighters showed even less emotion than Haz and I did. John, if he had not been so focused on getting to Juliette, would have been the most likely to express how upset he was at leaving them. But all he could think of was his daughter. He appeared completely unaffected by leaving the fighters in DC to fend for themselves.

In the next hour we dodged and weaved our way across the line of broken-down cars on the beltway. Now in suburbia, I stepped forward, taking the lead. In general I was better at navigation than Haz, just not in DC. Haz slowed his pace to allow John to go before him. I inhaled the smell of summer grasses and flowers, the birdsong stopping and restarting as we passed the flying creatures. We were far from rural America but already I felt calmer, my mind clearing with the sight of yards and houses instead of concrete buildings.

"How do people live in cities?" I half asked, half mumbled to myself.

"You're not a city girl?" John asked. By his tone he was being sarcastic.

"Too many people and buildings and cars, like giant ant colonies, with the ants all living on top of one another," I said.

"Are the people the ants?" John asked.

That sounded bad, but I said, "Yes. It increased my anxiety just being near all those buildings."

"You don't think all the exploding bullets had something to do with increasing your anxiety?" Haz joked.

"I've always been that way in cities," I said. "Even when no one was trying to kill me."

"I think it's what you get used to," Haz said. "If you had to live in the city, you would, and if I had to live in the country, I would. But I grew up in the city and was comfortable there, so I stayed until I couldn't stay any longer."

"I'm not sure I could ever get used to all that concrete," I said.

"What if vegetation returned?" Haz asked, more interested in my opinion of DC than I was.

I shrugged. "I guess if there was space to grow a garden and hunt nearby, then it wouldn't be so bad, especially if people stopped trying to kill me."

"My wife was like you," John said. "She was always taking the kids to the park, just to feel the grass and see the trees."

"How did you two meet?" Haz asked, his voice so kind it moved something inside me.

John never spoke of his family, only Juliette, and only now that he knew she was alive. He'd told us almost nothing about his wife and son.

John hesitated, but then answered. "I was working at my mom's law office the summer before I graduated from law school. Camille was dating one of the paralegals who worked there. She came to the office one day to meet him for lunch, and I couldn't stop staring at her. It was awful, but it was like I'd been struck by lightning."

Haz said, "Coming face to face with your destiny can do that to a person."

John laughed. "Yeah, but she thought I was a total creep and wouldn't come back to the office."

"So, a friend who worked there gave you her number," I said, predicting how their fairytale went. "She broke up with the other guy, you called her, and the rest is history."

John laughed again. "No, I went back to school. Went out on a few dates with a few different girls, nothing serious. Then I graduated and started working. Two years later I was at a restaurant with a friend, and Camille walked in with a different guy. She didn't notice me. I watched her the whole evening. I tried not to be weird about it. First, I was trying to see if she wore a ring. When I saw that she didn't, I was trying to decide if she was actually into the guy or just killing time with him."

"What did your friend do?" Haz asked, sounding amused.

"He tried to help me out," John said. "Alex and I had been friends since we were kids. We'd been through a lot together and the next many years would be no different." His thoughts were far away, remembering this friend who was likely dead.

He refocused, his voice rising at memories of that night. "Alex kept taking trips to the men's room to get a closer look or hear what they were saying. Our waitress probably thought he had some sort of medical issue," John said, entertained by the memory.

"Did you ask her out that night, while she was out with someone else?" I asked, surprised.

John chuckled and said, "No, that definitely would have creeped her out! I paid for her and her date's meal. I left my card with the waitress to give to Camille, hoping she would call me."

"But she wouldn't have known who you were," I said.

"It's a small town. My mom and I had the same last name. I was fairly certain she would know the name."

"She called the next morning?" Haz asked, getting into the story.

"She waited two months," John said.

"Two months!" Haz exclaimed.

"Two agonizingly long months," John repeated. "It seemed like forever back then."

"Why did she wait so long to call?" I asked.

"She figured I wanted to ask her out and she wanted to see how things turned out with the guy she was dating first. Once she realized he wasn't for her, she called me."

"It took you all over two years to get together?" Haz said.

"Closer to four," John said. "That's how life is. The best things are those you have to wait the longest for. Once we finally went out on a date, things went fairly quickly. I proposed six months later and we were married about seven months after that. Johnny arrived about two years later and Juliette, four years after that."

"Done after two, huh?" Haz joked.

"Not because we wanted to be," John said. "We were always open to more kids, but none ever came. We figured it was God's plan for our family. And it made sense. They could both be a handful, though in very different ways. Johnny needed us in lots of ways most kids eventually stopped needing their parents, and Juliette was independent in those respects, but needed us even more in other ways. Camille and I always felt we had been given very special children that needed a bit more than maybe some other kids, and so perhaps that was why God had given us only two."

I said, "My parents thought they were done after me, and then, eleven years later, my little brother was born, and then … I gave birth and they're raising her as well."

There was the subtlest of pauses. They both knew I had a child. I had told them, but this was the first time since the moment I had told them that I spoke of her.

"What's her name?" Haz asked.

I didn't look back at him. I didn't want to see his expression. "Quinn," I said.

"How old were you?" John asked kindly. "When she was born?"

"Fifteen." I answered in a way that I hoped told them I was done discussing Quinn and how she came to be in this world. I realized the double standard; I wanted John to share about his life and his family, but I didn't want to share about mine. The difference, I guessed, was that his children were conceived in love, and my child was not.

We weaved in and out of yards in silence. As more trees surrounded us and fewer houses appeared in the area, I relaxed. The trip to Raven Rock would be almost seventy miles. We could get there in three full days of walking. Closer to two days, if it was just me and Haz. But I wouldn't push us that hard. Now, safely out of DC, our pace could slow and we would still make better time because we didn't have to dodge new threats at every block.

When we entered the first patch of woods, I placed my palm on the uneven bark of a tree and said a silent prayer of thanksgiving. Haz watched me, but I didn't care. This was my sanctuary, where I felt most at home. It's probably why Saint Kateri Tekakwitha was one of my favorite saints. Living your life in the woods, praying. It would be what I chose for myself. The gun on my back grew heavy. I took my hand from the tree.

That simple quiet life might be what I chose for myself, but it was clearly not what had been chosen for me.

Six
BRIA

Three days had passed since we told everyone we loved that we were leaving. The sadness hung over me, suffocating even moments of joy. Leaving people I loved, not knowing if I would live long enough to see them again, was becoming common and it was hurting my soul. That sounded funny even in my thoughts, but it was true. I could feel it. The pain of leaving was causing me to create emotional distance between them and me. I felt it most with JP and my dad, the two I loved the most. I tried not to allow the distance in, but it protected me from the pain. JP was doing the same thing. When we told him we were leaving, he shoved Jonah and ran into the house. Since then he'd avoided us. If he did interact with us, it was with harsh words and furious glances.

My father, who had spent most of my life at an angry distance, was unwilling to allow it now. Even when I tried to create space, he was there beside me. In the last three days he left my side only to sleep and he did that reluctantly. We stood beside one another now, in silence, washing the clothes Jonah and I would take with us on our journey.

Much of our time together was spent in silence; we were both content with this. Actually, I preferred it. The times he spoke were times when he decided to bare his soul, and it was not always easy to hear, even of the good things. He never spoke of our life together after my mom's death. I was grateful for that; it wasn't a life either of us wanted to remember. We were emotionally dead, both alone, both in so much pain. I didn't blame him for my decisions. They were mine; I had made them and I took responsibility for them, but it would be wrong if I didn't acknowledge they were made because of him. Of how alone he had left me.

The truth was that when my mom and brother died, the man who now stood beside me, helping me wash clothes, became engrossed in his own grief. He turned hard and bitter. He was an awful man and a horrible father, and the complete truth was that if it had been him instead of Blaise's parents that shot those people, I would've felt nothing—certainly not surprise.

And yet here he was, trying desperately to be a father.

"How did you come back?" I asked, in the silence of splashing water.

He lifted his eyes to mine, his face so thin. He was once an attractive man. My high school friends always told me so, but they would not say that about him now, in this almost emaciated state.

"You look just like her," he said, a smile on his wrinkled face.

"I didn't know that until I saw the picture of her and Charlotte," I said, fighting the anger I felt at him never allowing me to see a picture of my mother.

He turned his eyes to the clothes and then back to me. "I couldn't look at you. It was like a stabbing pain in my heart every time I saw her staring back at me."

I focused on the clothes in my hand. I understood his reasoning, but it didn't make the hurt any less when my father said he couldn't bear to even see me.

"It only got worse as you got older, and then last summer you came home,"—he shook his head—"I mean, to visit me—as you said before last Thanksgiving, it was never a home for either of us."

I felt a twinge of guilt for the words I had texted him, telling him I didn't care where I was for Thanksgiving, as long as it wasn't with him.

He continued. "When you were there I saw you trying so hard to please Trent, trying so hard to earn his love. That's when I saw you for the first time in years. Your mom's beauty was not only in the shape of her face, it was in her soul. When I saw you and saw how much you didn't resemble her, something started to shift inside of me. But the real breaking point was when you told me you weren't coming home for Thanksgiving. The anger I felt was suddenly overrun by the memories of you as a child, of your beauty, and then of all we went through losing your mom and brother. That day, I cried for the first time in eighteen years."

I reached for his hand in the soapy water. His eyes were strong, not filled with tears as I expected.

"At that moment the fog that had filled my brain lifted and I understood what I'd done to you. I understood I was the one who took the joy from your soul. I was the reason you no longer resembled your mom. And that's when I promised to go to you," he said, his voice lightened. "Of course, I figured I would be driving to New York, not walking to North Carolina."

"You saved us that night," I said, remembering Mick's attack. The night we met Heath.

"You did the saving," he said, his damp fingers touching my arm.

"Do I look like her now?" I asked.

He smiled and said, "Exactly."

I kissed him on the cheek. What more could I do? How different our lives would've been if my mom had lived or if he hadn't left me. Neither of those things happened. All we were left with was this moment in time. A moment when he stood before me, fully present in my life, helping me hand-wash my husband's clothes.

"Thanks for coming back to me," I said.

"Thanks for allowing me to return."

Across the yard, Richard entered my line of sight. I watched him as he walked and my father did the same.

"I worry about him," Dad said quietly.

I turned to him. "Richard?"

He nodded. "His heart is closing. I can feel it more and more every day."

I mumbled, "I doubt murder is good for your soul."

"No, of course not, but it's more than that. Felicia did the same, but I don't sense the same misery in her as I do in him."

Dad was right. Miserable was a good word to describe Richard's general disposition. He had never been an overly joy-filled person. It was Felicia who used to balance him out and lift him up. She no longer did that. Perhaps because she only had enough for herself or because they were no longer as united as they once were.

"I can't imagine what happens in a marriage when murder is part of it," Dad said as he wrung out Jonah's shirt and hung it on the line.

I paused, watching Richard as he walked by Felicia. They smiled at one another. Hers was real, his was forced.

"They said they were going with us," I stated, as if that somehow proved they were okay.

"They are both very committed to Blaise and that is beautiful, but when your spouse, the person who is supposed to help lead you closer to God, is the very one who pulls you from him, ..." He shook his head. "That would be a hard thing for a Christian marriage to come back from."

"Why a Christian marriage?"

"I guess I shouldn't limit it to a Christian marriage, but those are the marriages that should most closely emulate Christ's love for his Church. I suppose any marriage where there is a dying of self for the other, a true continual and mutual gift of self, is what I'm speaking of. Those are the marriages where the effect of sin is felt most acutely because love and sin cannot coexist. Other unions that are based on mutual selfishness can withstand sin because neither party actually cares about the other. They are there for money, status, beauty, or some other thing their partner gives and they take—as long as those things remain, they remain. Once they're gone, so are they."

"Blaise's parents were never like that," I said.

"That's obvious," Dad said. "Just as it's obvious that sin is trying to tear them apart."

Richard was in the barn now, no longer visible from where we stood. Felicia sat beside Sara, who was carving wood that Eli was using for the tabernacle.

"Is it always the man who falls hardest?" I asked, though I probably shouldn't have. I didn't care. "I think about you and Mom, and Richard and Felicia. Not that

Richard did any worse than Felicia, but he's handling it worse, and maybe if you had died, Mom would've done the same thing as you, but—"

"Never," he said, interrupting with force. "She never for a second would've been anything less to you than the best mother possible."

We were silent for a moment. As much as he didn't always love me, he had always loved my mother, and something about that struck me as right. Not that he shouldn't have loved me too, but that loving my mom, his wife, should have been and was his top priority.

His body relaxed and his voice calmed. "Men are so often filled with pride. And pride is the deadliest of sins. Maybe that's why we fall more or harder."

"You think it was pride that broke you and is breaking Richard?" I asked, not understanding.

"I think that has something to do with it. Until your mom and brother passed, I believed I had control over life. In that moment I learned I had none, but I refused to accept it, so I turned my back on the truth and made myself into a god."

I thought back to the way he was revered and feared. He had tremendous power and an obscene bank account.

"Richard wasn't like that," I said. "He was kind and giving. People liked him, Blaise loved him." I stopped; I hadn't meant to say all the things my father wasn't.

"I was once kind and giving and peopled liked me and you adored me," he said, his eyes grim. "It's easy to be those things when life is going the way you want it to go. It becomes harder when your world comes crashing down. When my world ended, I became someone who forgot everything I valued and did what was easiest. Richard did the same. Now he's faced with that truth, the same way I was faced with it. The difference, though, is that he tarnished Felicia's soul as well as his own. And without extreme humility, he will lose her."

"I hope you're wrong," I said, as Blaise and Josh went into the barn.

"I hope I am too, but I'm not." My father spoke the words plainly. He had reached a point in his life when wisdom came as easily as pride had once come.

"How did you become so wise?" I asked, aware that this was not how he had always been.

He stretched his wrinkled hand out. All muscles and fat were gone, only bones and skin remaining. "Wisdom comes from silence. When we get rid of the noise, we allow God in, and when we allow God in, wisdom can't help but follow. Plus, I'm old as dirt."

"You're no older than Charlotte and Quint," I said, though even as I spoke the words, I accepted I was wrong. My father had aged a decade since the light. It was as if all the pain he'd been feeling on the inside finally started to show on the outside and he looked like he was closer to Nonie's age than any of the others.

"Maybe not in human years, but in dog years I'm as old as dirt," he said, winking, making a joke of the truth.

I laughed. "I'm glad you came back to me," I said, bumping his hip with mine.

"Me too. Now you have to do the same. Come back here as soon as you find East."

"What if I don't make it back?" I said, biting my lip, fear overwhelming me.

He took my hand in his. "Honey, you will be back and you will have a long and happy life with Jonah by your side."

"You can't know that," I said, and sniffed.

"Perhaps not, but it doesn't change the fact that I do. I am exceedingly wise, remember," he said, staring into my eyes and daring me not to smile.

But behind the joke there was truth. He believed his words and his belief brought me peace.

Seven
BRIA

Our bags were packed and in the yard.

"I'm going inside to find Dad," I said to Jonah and the others who were gathered.

It was still dark, and my father was no longer an early riser. He was now the first to bed, the last to wake, and often slept in the middle of the day if the chores were light or the rains were strong.

He was in the kitchen sitting at the table, eyes confused, back bent. He looked even older than he had yesterday.

When he saw me, his eyes cleared and his back straightened.

"How are you feeling this morning?" I asked, aware this was the first morning I'd seen him so soon after he awoke.

Typically, Jonah and I made our way to the main house much later than this, and by then my dad had been up and active for some time. Now, though, he was stiff and sore from sleep, unable to hide it from me.

He said, "A little sore, but I'll be fine in a few minutes."

"Is this how you feel most mornings?" I asked, trying to hide the concern.

"Getting old is not for the weak." He laughed, making a joke, and it would've been a joke if Nonie, who was in her eighties, said it, but it wasn't funny coming from a man the same age as Quint and Charlotte.

"Here, let me pour you some tea," I said as I lifted the kettle and filled a ceramic mug. I handed it to him, grazing his fingers as I did so.

"Your fingers are like ice," I said, placing my hands on his bare arms. "And your arms," I added with concern.

"It's the morning," he said. "I'm always cold in the morning."

"Didn't you say that last night about the evenings?"

"Hmm, I may have," he said in a joking tone. "I'm plenty hot in the middle of the day."

"Aren't we all," I said.

"Where's Jonah?" Dad asked, changing the subject.

"Outside, with the others. I came in here to find you."

"Are you leaving soon?"

"Yes," I said, not allowing my words to connect with my emotions.

He placed his tea on the table. "Then I'm going to get as many hugs as I can."

I leaned my head on his shoulder as we hugged, his bones protruding through the thin strip of muscle. Had he lost the weight he had gained since finding us?

"Are you feeling okay, Dad?" I asked, suddenly aware that though it was summer, he had almost no color on his pale face.

A hint of something came over his eyes, then it was gone. Behind him the door opened and Jonah came in.

Dad turned to face him, not answering my question.

"Are you ready?" Jonah asked me.

"Yes," I lied. I would never be ready.

Dad offered me his hand and I gratefully took it. We walked together through the door. Jonah squeezed my shoulder as we passed him. In the yard I saw everyone else I loved. Even Fulton and Talin stood nearby, grazing at the edge of the garden. As we approached, Talin lifted her head and trotted toward us. She reached me before I reached the others. Her head pushed against my body as I wrapped my arms around her neck.

"I'm sorry," I said to her. "I don't want to leave, but we'll come home soon. JP will take care of you until we get back."

She stomped her foot and pushed her neck against me. She didn't want me to leave.

"Come on now," Dad said, petting Talin. "If I can survive Bria leaving, so can you."

Talin huffed, as if to say "Speak for yourself." Dad held her as I left them and went to the others.

They were already hugging, saying their goodbyes. It was my turn to begin the process, but I didn't want to begin. Jonah had reminded me the previous night that there was no reason to think of these goodbyes as anything more than "I will see you in a few weeks." It would be months, but I didn't argue with him on that point. He was mostly right.

It was possible we might never make it home, but it was not overly likely. We'd survived this trip before, when we had no idea what to expect. Now we knew. Our trip home had been far easier than our trip out because we had an understanding of what paths to take and what sorts of things to avoid. We'd gotten good at recognizing the signs that cities were near. When we saw houses becoming more frequent and roads becoming wider, with fewer potholes, we changed our routes. That meant we traveled more miles—but avoided danger.

Maria came to me and used her one free arm to pull me in for an affectionate hug. Kissing me on the cheek, she said, "Be safe, darling."

Everyone was "darling" to her.

"I will, and take care of your own little darlings," I said, hugging Isabelle, who was in her arms. They were kind children being raised by kind, hardworking parents.

Other than Heath's long nose, there were no similarities to Mick.

"I will. They are my joy. I'm so grateful we're here with your family, where they can be safe and free."

"Me too," I said, so very grateful we hadn't killed Heath when he attacked us.

They added so much to our family. Now, with so many of us leaving, they would move back into the main house. It was safer that way, for everyone. Knowing they would all be together under one roof brought me a sense of peace.

Juliette stood before me, Astrea by her side. She opened her arms and I took her in mine.

"You're almost as tall as me," I said.

She moved her head up and down against my shoulder. From the first day of our announcement, she had said she was coming with us. I reminded her that Haz had told her, no matter what, to stay here, but that had done nothing other than to make her miss Haz and East.

Ultimately, Sara had changed Juliette's mind, telling her bluntly that she was needed here. Nonie, JP, Quinn, my dad, Isabelle, Max, Astrea's future puppies—all of them were mouths to feed. Each contributed, but not as much as they ate. If anything happened to Sage, the numbers would be even more out of balance. Juliette's skills with a rifle rivaled those of Blaise, Richard, and Quint, and they could not lose her too.

After that talk, she agreed to stay. Which pleased everyone—even her, I think. She had done exactly what East had asked, become a big sister to JP and Quinn. She was a granddaughter to Nonie, a friend to Sara, Sage, and the rest of my friends, and an extreme help to Charlotte and Quint. She was loved and admired by all, and as much as her staying was useful, it was also a gift to each of us to know she would be safe and would be helping to keep the rest of those we loved safe.

"Please help my dad," I whispered. "He doesn't look well."

She turned her head to face him. "I will try," she said. With her arms still wrapped around me, she said, "Be careful." Astrea whined at her side.

"I will," I said, squeezing her tight as Quinn somberly ambled toward us.

"Bria," Quinn said as she fell against my hips, "bring my sister home! Don't you dare let her stay in that awful place again."

Quinn was like a recorder, repeating everything she heard. These were Nonie's words.

"I will do my best," I said.

"That's weak," she replied.

This expression she got from Josh.

I squeezed her. "I promise I will do my very very best, but your sister is a lot like you. Neither one of you likes listening to what other people ask you to do."

She grinned, saying, "That's why she loves me the most. I'm just like her."

"You are just like her," Quint said. "Heaven help us all." He shook his head as she beamed up at him with pride.

"Take care of yourself and your husband," he said, pulling me into a hug.

"I will," I said.

He and Charlotte both did that; they no longer referred to Jonah as their son, but instead as my husband.

Charlotte came behind Quint. "I'll miss you so much," she said through tears. She couldn't keep from crying at moments like this.

"I'll miss you too," I said, holding her. She had become so much of a mom to me.

Two days ago, I had given her the note East wrote to Quinn. I didn't tell her what it was. Only that if, for some reason I wasn't able to, that she should give it to Quinn when she was older. I didn't say it was from East; I didn't have to. She took it and held the folded paper against her heart. Then kissed it before placing it gingerly in a drawer in her bedroom.

"Take care of my dad," I whispered to her. "I'm worried about him."

She held me as she sucked in air. Then loosened her arms, her lips turned up in a smile. "Don't worry about your dad. He'll be better soon." She blinked and turned away, moving on to say goodbye to Jonah.

So, it wasn't my imagination. He wasn't doing well. Was he simply worried about me or was there something more?

I would think about that later. Sara was in front of me, her arms wrapping around me, tears streaming.

"You've turned into such a softy," I teased, as she fell against me, crying.

She sniffed and laughed. "This is who I've always been on the inside, a big ol' squishy mess."

"You're beautiful, in kind of a gross way," I said as she wiped snot onto her shirt sleeve.

She laughed and hugged me again. "Thanks. You're beautiful, not in a gross way."

"Good luck with Sage," I said.

Sara nodded.

"Sage is tough," Sage said, throwing an arm around me from behind.

I turned, wrapping an arm around her and another around Sara.

"You are ridiculously tough and your baby will be too," I said.

She put her hand on her belly. "Let's hope. Of course, you'll be here to meet him or her when it's born," she said with a tone of commanding expectation.

"I'm sure I will be."

"You better be, or you'll be freezing," Sara said. "You remember last Thanksgiving, right? Storms could be even worse this year."

"I think I could live a million years and never forget that day," I said.

Sara was right. The snow would be here half as soon as Sage's baby, and we would either be home or fighting for our lives against Mother Nature.

"We will definitely be here long before your baby is," I said with confidence.

"Um-hm, you better. He or she is gonna need Auntie Bria," Sage said, arms folded, trying to appear tough.

I pulled her to me. "I can't wait to meet my little niece or nephew. Don't let your sister make you sit and rest too much," I said, grinning at Sara.

"I will make her sit and rest as much as I possibly can," Sara said, slipping her hand into mine.

Blaise came beside me. Sage stepped away as if knowing this time was for just the three of us.

"I can't believe I'm letting you two go off on an adventure without me," Sara said.

"Not exactly the fun sort of adventure," Blaise said.

"No, but it's the without me part that's so hard. I haven't been away from you guys for more than a week in, like, four years. I don't know how I'm going to survive without my best friends."

Josh appeared behind Sara. "*You* are going to survive great. *You* have running water and a house and a bed and, by the time we get back, you'll have a working windmill. And, between Juliette's skills with a rifle and the breeding rabbits and hogs, you'll have plenty of meat. *We*, on the other hand, will have none of those things. So, it is *we*, not *you*, that you need to be concerned about surviving."

"Josh, you are too sweet to die, and your wife is too tough," Sara said, taking his face in her hand and kissing him on the cheek.

"Let's hope you're right about that," he said, with smooshed cheeks that made his voice sound even sweeter than it already was.

"She is," Blaise said, winking at Josh.

"Take care of Sage," I said, my voice low so Sage couldn't hear. "She's as stubborn as you, so you'll have to force her not to work too hard."

"She is nowhere near as stubborn as me," Sara teased. "Besides, Nonie is far more stubborn than either of us, and with you two gone, all of her great-grandbaby–wanting energy will be focused on Sage. Once she hits the third trimester, Sage'll be lucky if Nonie lets her pour a glass of water."

We laughed because she wasn't exaggerating. Nonie's desire for more tiny mouths to feed was intense and the word "stubborn" didn't begin to describe her. I supposed you didn't get to your mid-eighties by letting life have its way. You only made it that far if you had enough fight in you to make it. Nonie, I had no doubt, had enough fight to make it to well past one hundred.

Sara followed my gaze and released my hand. "I love you," she said.

"I love you too," I said, giving her one last hug before moving toward the goodbyes I was dreading most.

JP stood beside my father. Both of their faces were streaked with dirt and tears: JP's face, young and smooth, my father's, old and weathered. I loved them both. I went first to JP and pulled him to the side, away from my dad.

"Will you do me a favor while I'm gone?" I asked.

He said nothing.

"Will you take care of my dad? Make sure he's eating and not working too hard? It worries me how thin he is."

"It would be better if you stayed here and took care of him yourself," JP said in a mopey tone.

"JP, you know I can't do that. I belong with your brother, and we need to find your sister."

"My sister can take care of herself. She doesn't need him or anyone else rescuing her," he said, this time with anger.

"You're definitely right about that, but what if it was Quinn and what if you two were grown up and not fighting all the time? What if you left her somewhere that wasn't safe and you did it because she asked you to? Even though she's an adult and can make her own decisions, wouldn't you still be her big brother and wouldn't you want to make sure she was safe?"

"Quinn is so mean, no one would dare mess with her," he said, his arms crossed.

I kissed the top of his head. "I love you, JohnPaul."

"But you love Jonah more," he said, pouting.

"I love him differently. He's my husband, and haven't you been taught that husbands should put their wives first and wives should put their husbands first?"

"That's not what he's doing! He's putting his sister first. If he was putting his wife first, you wouldn't be leaving."

His words stung because a part of me believed them.

I said, "You don't stop loving your family just because you get married."

"You said you would be here when the first apple was ripe," JP said, his anger replaced by sadness.

"I was here for the blackberries," I said, trying to appease him.

"Blackberries don't count," he said, arms folded tight against his chest.

"Apples last longer. Keep some in the spring house, and I'll be back before the last one rots," I said.

"If you're not back in time, you'll have to eat a rotten apple," JP said, his face scrunching in delighted disgust.

"All the more reason for me to get going," I said, my hand resting on his neck.

"Fine," he said, opening his arms and allowing me to hug him.

"I love you," I said.

"I love you too," he said, holding me so tight I could barely breathe. He relaxed his hold, and I kissed the top of his head.

He released me and turned to his brothers, who were saying goodbye to their parents. I couldn't imagine being Charlotte. Three of her children would now be gone from her, into a world she never wanted for them. Eli had been the one, before, that I counted on to help the others deal with the pain of our leaving, and he too was leaving. Another one of Charlotte's children leaving. She was crying as Jonah hugged her. Eli and Quint were sniffing as they shook hands and then embraced.

My pack sat beside my father's legs. He lifted it and handed it to me.

"Are you trying to get rid of me, Dad?" I said, relieved to have something lighthearted to say.

He shook his head. "Never, but goodbyes are hard and I don't like them. I've never liked them."

"Me either," I said. "I never know what to say, not really."

"It just hurts," he said.

"Yeah, it does," I said, staring into his eyes.

Something was there that I didn't understand. Something I couldn't see. He blinked, and I lost it. Whatever it was that I almost saw was gone.

"The thing to remember is no goodbye is forever, no matter how long they're for," he said.

"What do you mean?"

"Think about your mom and brother. We haven't seen them in so long, but we will, we will see them again someday. And all the suffering I went through, and put you through, it was unnecessary because I will be with them again someday. I caused us so much senseless pain," he said.

"It's all right, Dad. I've forgiven you," I said, wanting to make sure he released any guilt he felt over the pain he'd caused me. His hand felt smooth in mine.

"I'm so grateful that you've forgiven me," he said. "But do you understand how unnecessary it was? I wasted all those years in agony and putting you through the same, for no reason. Life is so short. I'll be with your mom and brother soon enough and all that pain will fall away."

I felt both confused and worried. I understood by his words that he now believed that when he died, he would choose to go to heaven, something he was concerned about even a few weeks ago as he came to terms with the truth of his past behavior. But I didn't understand why he was telling me this now, and it bothered me that he did.

"Are you telling me you're dying?" I asked, searching his eyes for the truth.

He laughed. "How on earth did you get that out of what I just said? Here I was, trying to explain the importance of living in the moment, recognizing that life is short, and that eventually all the pain goes away. It was supposed to be something positive, but I can tell I've upset you. I'm sorry," he said, touching his hand to my face.

"You haven't upset me," I lied. I lifted my hand to his, holding it against my face. "I'm not leaving forever, only a few weeks. I promised JP I would be back before the last apple rotted or I would have to eat one—and I don't want to eat a rotten apple."

"That definitely does not sound appetizing," he said as his laugh turned into a cough.

"Are you feeling all right?" I asked.

He cleared his throat. "Just allergies," he answered, keeping his eyes from mine. "It's been a few days since the rain washed away all the dust, and this dry wind isn't helping."

I stared at him. There was something more.

"It's time for you to leave, sweetie," my dad said, his gaze beyond me.

I turned. The others stood in a loose cluster.

"I love you so much," he said, his voice choking with sadness.

"I love you too," I said, throwing my arms around him. His body was so thin and frail. "Dad, promise me you'll eat while I'm gone."

"I always eat," he said.

"You always eat, but you don't always eat enough. You call it fasting. I call it starving. We have plenty of meat now and the garden is doing great. You can eat your fill and you won't be taking food from any other mouth, so please eat," I begged, my fingertips almost touching as they wrapped around his frail arm.

"I promise to eat my fill," he said. "You should go now."

"I love you," I said, hugging him one more time.

"I love you, my darling girl, now and forever."

My skin turned cold, his words reminding me of those my mother wrote to me the day she died.

"Go now," he said, his fingers gently touching the side of my face.

I opened my mouth to speak, but no words came. Instead I kissed him on the cheek and ran to Jonah, who was waiting for me.

I slipped my hand into his. Turning once as we entered the trees, I saw Charlotte had her arms around my dad, watching us leave their lives yet again. Quint's arm circled around Nonie. She waved when she saw me. I forced myself to wave back. Sara held Quinn, Sage and her tiny growing belly beside them. Quinn was crying, but Sara was encouraging her to blow kisses to us. Maria and Heath were there, each holding one of their kids. Franklin stood beside them and barked twice. On the far side, near the horses, were Astrea and Juliette, a rifle on her shoulder. She reminded me so much of Blaise and East. She was no longer the scared silent girl; she was a brave, capable woman who would help protect and feed those I loved.

"They're going to be okay," I said.

"Yes," Jonah said as he squeezed my hand. "And we are too."

I hoped we were both right.

Eight
EAST

I was about to break my promise to John. Part of me thought I should feel bad about that, but it was a small part, growing smaller by the moment as the distant hill the town sat on came into sight.

John stopped. "Why are we here?" he asked, his voice angry.

He felt betrayed. I didn't blame him.

"You promised we would go straight to Raven Rock from DC, and from there straight to my daughter." His voice thick with doubt and fear.

I placed my hands on the straps of my pack to lift them from my shoulders. The day had been long, longer than expected. "This is not far out of the way and it's a safe place for us to spend the night."

"You don't get to decide where we go without asking the rest of us," John said, furious.

I kept my tone even, saying, "Actually, I do. That's what the person who leads does. They make decisions. The decisions they believe are best."

"You aren't our leader, you're our navigator," John growled.

Haz stepped forward. "East did what she thought was right, and I agree with her. Spending the night at the town makes sense. It's barely out of the way and it offers safety while we sleep and food when we wake."

I hadn't discussed my decision to take us here with Haz either, but I never doubted he would agree with my logic because it was in fact logical. John, on the other hand—I was sure this would be his response, which was why I had not told him.

"We keep going," John said.

"You're thinking too much with your heart," I countered. "Your impatience could get us killed, and then Juliette would never see you again."

His face reddened. No one liked to be told they were being too emotional.

Haz placed his hand on John's shoulder in a gesture of friendship.

John calmed and turned to face him.

"What East meant to say is if we don't go to the town, we'll be forced to hunt, which will delay us far more than this subtle detour has, and in town we can each sleep. No one will need to be on watch. All of us being well fed and well rested before getting to Raven Rock is a good thing."

"She should have told us," John said.

"Yes, she should have," Haz conceded.

I crossed my arms in defiance. "And if I had, what would have changed?"

"Nothing," Haz said, "but that's not the point. It was wrong of you to decide this for us."

I felt my face flush with anger. "I made the right decision and am being criticized for it."

"It wasn't your decision to make." Haz held out his hand to calm me down. "Not alone. That's all we're saying. John's right. You're the navigator, not the one in charge of us, and we should've been consulted."

"I don't need to listen to this," I said as I turned and started toward the open fields in front of the town.

I went on, not bothering to see if the others were coming. Clearly, they didn't need me to tell them where to go. It wasn't my fault John could only think of Juliette. I didn't blame him. He had thought she was dead and now he knew she lived. I was sure the miles and hours we spent heading north, away from her, must be a source of tremendous suffering for him, but the truth was Juliette was safe. I could feel it. She was at my home with my family. She was well fed, protected, cared for, loved. She didn't know her father was alive; she wasn't counting the minutes, as he was, until she saw him again. This delay was painful for John but not for Juliette, and so we'd take the time needed to reach Raven Rock safely. And once we were there we would again take the time needed to learn, or possibly—if it was as we hoped and Jael and Ash were already there—to teach them what we could about DC and those in charge.

As I crossed the open field, I heard Haz and John behind me. I didn't turn. I focused instead on the steep hill in front of us. I didn't like that we were leaving a trail to the town through the tall summer grasses, but its existence wasn't a secret and it wasn't defenseless. Even now, someone from town was undoubtedly watching us approach. I tried to see them at the lookout spot, but it was well hidden. Exactly as it should be.

The sun set as we began the climb up the hill. A gray glow colored the air and a sense of peace warmed my soul. This was the feeling I had as a young child when I came home after being away at my grandparents' home or a friend's house. It was the feeling of home.

As the barking and snarling dogs came toward us, the peace left, replaced by fear. It was no longer terror; that was an improvement. I allowed the fear to wash over me as I reminded myself that HoneyBee and Jasper would never hurt me. They protected all those in the town and their puppy, Astrea, was now with those I loved. These dogs were a part of my life, a good part of it. They were not Wrath. They would fight to protect me, and I would fight to protect them.

They came into view and the snarling and barking stopped. They could smell us. HoneyBee bounded toward me. With hesitation, she came closer. Could she sense I was uneasy? She gently pushed her head against my thigh. I shivered, but forced my hand to touch her silky head.

"Hey, girl," I said softly. She lifted her head against my hand as if to say "Welcome back."

"Man, I love this dog," Haz said as he and Jasper were wrapped in a full-body hug.

I laughed at the sight and their resulting tumble to the ground. There was something about men … they never really grew up. It was … endearing to see Haz, so strong and independent, fall to the ground, playing with a dog.

"Becca said you three were on your way up," Gus said as he made his way down the slope, toward us.

John stood behind me, crouched onto his knees, petting HoneyBee. He stood and went to Gus. I was glad Gus was the one to meet us. He and John had become good friends the last time we were here. I hoped seeing him would help John understand we didn't come here to upset him; it was for the best, whether or not he agreed with it.

"Glad y'all are back," Gus said as he offered Haz his hand to help him stand. "It's not the same around here without all of you."

"We aren't back for long," John said, his voice giddy.

Gus turned to him in surprise. "Did you find good news?" he asked, his tone hopeful.

"My daughter's alive," John said, choking on the words.

Gus stopped and stared at him, his eyes wide. "She's alive?" he said as he held John's shoulders, the two men staring at each other.

"Juliette," Haz said softly.

"Juliette?" Gus said, and gasped, wide eyes going from John to Haz and back to John.

"She's my baby girl," John said, tears of pride and joy and sorrow filling his eyes.

"The beautiful silent girl that my son had a crush on is your daughter?" Gus said, still holding tight to John's shoulders.

"She's always been quiet," John acknowledged, though I could tell the thought of her silence brought him pain. He didn't say anything more.

"I'm quiet," Gus said, teasing. "She was silent, but beautiful inside and out." He paused. "I can see it," Gus said, staring at John. "You have her eyes."

John nodded and, sniffing, said, "We're going to her. After we go to Raven Rock, we'll go to my Juliette, and maybe ..." His voice choked as the tears fell.

"Maybe she'll know where to find your wife and son," Gus said, his voice filled with tears as he pulled John into a hug.

Before the light struck, men didn't cry, or at least I never saw it. Only once did I see my father cry and that was the day I almost died. Now they cried all the time. I used to wonder if they didn't feel things the same, if that was the reason they didn't cry. Watching Gus comfort John, and all the other tears I'd seen before and after this moment, since the giant lights in the sky, made me understand they felt things similarly to how women did. Before the light they simply hid their emotions better.

I didn't blame them.

Crying made you vulnerable. I hated crying in front of people. But it took work to keep the tears in, and in a world where our bodies and minds were constantly pushed beyond what we imagined possible, there was little energy to be spent hiding emotions. Especially when it came to love and loss.

The children growing up now would be used to this world; they would be stronger and they would know loss from the earliest of ages. They would not cry like we did, and the children they raised would be even harder.

As I watched the comfort and support Gus showed John, I felt sadness. Emotion was good, expressing emotion was good. I didn't want our world to evolve into people who couldn't or wouldn't cry, even if it did show we were vulnerable. Being vulnerable wasn't bad, I decided, when shared with the right people.

John being vulnerable with Gus strengthened their friendship and united them. Seeing John's tears made me want to work harder to get him home faster. No, showing emotion was definitely not all bad.

The sun was long gone by the time we entered the town, which meant most people were already in their huts. Burning trees to provide light, but not heat, was a waste and the people here were far from wasteful. The few people we saw were on their way to bed. We exchanged waves and hugs, but that was all. Days were long, especially during the summer. When night came, it was time to sleep.

Gus said, "Y'all can bunk with me and Thomas tonight. May have to scoot some dogs out of the way, but that's all right. Thomas and me have raised beds now, so most of 'em sleep beneath us, anyway. East, you can have my bunk."

"Gus, I'm not going to take your bed," I said, unsurprised by his offer. He was someone who would literally give a person the shirt off his back.

"Right there, that's why you're single," Gus said, winking at me. "You've got to let a man be a man. You gotta let him sacrifice for you. It makes a guy feel good to do something nice for a beautiful woman."

He loved giving me a hard time. He didn't know about my past, only that I never dated and he told me that was a tragedy, and I shouldn't deny all the young men around me of my company.

I shrugged. "If you really want to sleep on the dirt, then I won't keep you from it."

"We have enough blankets. None of us will be in the dirt," he said. "Thomas is sleeping, but that doesn't matter. That boy can sleep through anything."

The young dogs lifted their heads as we entered the hut. When their parents entered, they lowered their heads and went back to sleep. Thomas's breathing was peaceful and rhythmic. I took off my shoes and slid onto the raised bed. It was harder than the ground would've been, but it was nicer at the same time: a wooden platform with leaves and grasses on top, covered with a quilt, and a second quilt for use as a blanket. Gus's wife had made both quilts.

Gus was the first to fall asleep, followed by John, and lastly, Haz. I turned to my side and pulled the quilt up to my chin. I thought of Gus's wife, and I thanked her in my heart for the quilts I now used.

As I lay in the dark, listening to the quiet snores of the three men, one boy, and the pack of dogs, Gus's words echoed in my mind. He was joking while being honest too. He believed I was single because I was too independent. He was wrong, of course. I was single because I was even more scared of men, or the thought of dating a man, than I was of dogs. But I wondered if maybe I was too … something, not independent, that was a good thing, but something else. As irritated as I was at Haz and John, they were right. I should've asked them or at least told them we were coming here before they discovered it for themselves. I would be furious if either of them had led me somewhere I didn't agree to go, no matter how logical it was.

Haz rolled in his sleep, his breathing and features softening. One of the dogs whined and stretched. I closed my eyes, surprised I would sleep so close to so many dogs. And more surprised I would sleep so close to so many men. My body relaxed as my mind accepted that here, in this hut, with these dogs and these men, I had nothing to fear.

Nine
BRIA

Our first day was spent in silence as the reality of the choice we had made sunk in. All of us had left safety and all but Felicia and Richard left behind someone, or many someones, that we loved. No words any of us spoke could ease the pain we felt, so we didn't speak other than to provide basic information about the direction we were going and the path we were taking. At night I lay beside Jonah, his arms wrapped protectively around me. His body pressing against mine, this was the first time I felt peace since we left our home.

"I'm sorry I made us leave," he whispered into the darkness.

I rolled over to face him. My fingers grazed his clean-shaven face. "Do you think I regret leaving?" I asked.

"I'm not sure, but I regret making you."

"You didn't make me or anyone else do anything. We came because we love East." I paused. "Or maybe felt too guilty to stay." That was the only reason we could guess for Richard and Felicia joining us. That and wanting to be near Blaise.

"Yeah, but if I hadn't said I needed to go, the rest of you wouldn't have left. It was my idea and the weight of it rests on me."

"If you hadn't said you needed to go, you wouldn't be the man I married, and I'm very proud to be that man's wife. Besides, we have free will. Josh, Blaise, her parents, Eli, we all made up our own minds and we know the way home. Our lives are not your responsibility and your feeling guilty is only going to make you less effective and put us at risk."

He kissed me and lay on his back. I shifted my head to his shoulder, my leg over his.

After a minute or so, he said, "You're right."

"I always am," I said softly.

He laughed and strengthened his arm around me, pulling my body closer.

This was the biggest change since we were married. Not the physical closeness, the emotional closeness. Jonah told me of his fears and uncertainties. This vulnerability made me love him even more. Before we married, there was an aspect of untouchableness to him, of being almost too good to be true. Now I saw all of him and loved all of him, not only the shining parts, but the dull, rough parts too.

How it was possible for me to love him more than I did on our wedding day, I didn't understand, but I did.

Every day I felt my love for him grow, and he told me the same was true for him. It made sense to me now, how people who spent a lifetime loving one another ended up looking similar to each other. Their cells were merely doing what their spirits were doing, growing more and more in sync every moment.

Across the camp, Eli sat on watch. There was enough moonlight for me to see the strand of beads that hung from his hand. I wondered how it was for a priest or for whatever Sara was. Would they meld into the one they loved most? Would they grow more and more to look and act like Christ? Yes, I was sure that was the goal.

Beside me, Jonah's breath shifted to sleep. It was his goal too, I supposed. He loved me, but he loved God more. At first this bothered me, to be second, but that was before that night in the old church, before I understood how deeply he loved his Lord. Now it was simply one more aspect of my husband that I adored. And it occurred to me that if Jonah grew to be more like God, and I grew to be more like Jonah, then perhaps, in some roundabout way, I would grow to be more like God.

My eyes closed, and opened far too soon. My body ached as the sun rose. Sleeping on the ground was a special talent, one I apparently had lost in the last few months of sleeping comfortably on our homemade mattress.

"I think I slept on a rock," Josh said, rubbing his hip as he and Blaise sat up.

Blaise stretched her back as I pushed myself into a sitting position. Jonah sat up beside me, his short hair sticking up. He ran his hand through it to comb it down.

"How was the night?" he asked as Eli sat straighter, stretching and yawning as he did so.

"Uneventful," Eli answered, loosening the beads from around his wrist and tucking them into his bag.

Richard and Felicia were also sitting. They had slept near one another, but not as close as Jonah and I or Blaise and Josh. I thought of my dad's words and I wondered what happens to people who spend half of their life in sync and then become jarringly out of sync? Would their spirits and bodies pull away from the other's?

The day was warm and my legs were sore. That didn't matter; they would feel better soon. We each gathered our pack and reluctantly began the day's journey. Blaise and Josh led the way, with Richard and Felicia near them. They all wanted to be near Blaise, but it was only Josh that Blaise wanted to be near.

Eli walked beside Jonah and me, whistling softly as loose clouds blocked the morning sun. The tune was familiar. I listened as he continued, and recognized it as one of those he chose to be sung during the Sunday Mass. It spoke of Christian joy, but sounded more like a song a slave may have sung. The slow pace was perfect for heavy work and long walks. It fit today, and I found myself humming along. The tune helped the miles go faster.

"Stop," Felicia said as she pointed at the ground.

Richard stopped and stared. Josh and Blaise turned, each instinctively reaching for their weapon.

"What is it?" Jonah asked as we approached her.

Richard knelt with one knee to the ground. "Tire tracks," he said.

My body tensed as I swung around trying to find the source of the imprinted dirt. I pulled my weapon and crouched lower.

"Get down," Jonah said to Eli, the only one among us that didn't understand what was happening.

We were in a field, at the center of which stood a dilapidated barn. By the looks of its weathered, rough, and gray boards, it had been abandoned for decades.

At our feet the grass was short and trampled. Where there was dirt the tire imprints filled the space. Why hadn't we noticed the trampled grass? I spun around—it was trampled everywhere.

This land had once been farmland that had turned back into forest maybe ten or twenty years ago. There were trees, but they were young and thin. Grass and dirt covered most of the land near the barn and when it transitioned from saplings to open grass, the flatness of the grass didn't stand out because there were no taller grasses to compare it to.

My heart started to race. Around the barn the ground was dirt, not grass, as it should've been if it was abandoned. Inside was no different. Through giant swatches of missing roof, sunlight poured into the barn. Tall grasses should fill the ground where the sunlight glowed, but it didn't. There was only dirt around and in the barn. This place was not abandoned.

"Back up," Richard whispered, gun in hand.

Jonah and I turned, keeping our backs to our friends, searching for a place that could keep us from being seen. The trees were too small to hide behind and the shrubs too few.

"Faster," Richard yelled.

In the distance, dust rose into the sky. I thanked God we were on the back side of the barn, away from the entrance, as the dust cloud continued toward us, bringing with it the sounds of motors. We approached a mound of piled earth, large enough to hide all of us, with grass growing on top of it. Perhaps it was left here all those years ago when this place was abandoned. I dove behind it, feeling great gratitude to whomever had brought in this mound of dirt and then forgotten about it.

"Harvesters," Jonah whispered.

I closed my eyes as the machines got louder and louder.

"They're so close to home," I said, feeling sick at the realization of how near they were to JP and my dad.

Felicia said, "I never dreamt they would make it this far south."

"Do you know them?" Eli asked. He could tell by the responses of the six of us that whoever these people were, they were feared and not unknown.

Josh answered, "We know people like them."

"They work for DC," Jonah explained. "They bring them slaves and food." He did not elaborate and say Richard and Felicia had once been part of them.

Eli's expression fell, but in a way that told me such darkness was not unknown to him. He was not surprised that slaves existed, he was not surprised that slave traffickers existed, and he was not even surprised they were here. His eyes were hard yet compassionate. He had an expression of knowledge and understanding, of disgust and sadness. He was not, as I might have imagined a priest to be, naïve to the darkness.

"Any time they use trucks like that, they're transporting," Richard said, inching toward the edge of the mound.

"Do you think they have slav—people in the truck?" Josh asked.

"I'm not sure," Richard said. "This is nowhere near the camp we were at, so I'm not sure if they are on their way down or back up to DC."

"We'll need to move closer," Blaise said.

"Closer?" I asked.

"To find out if there are people in the truck," she answered.

My stomach churned. She was right, of course. If they had slaves, we had to free them. But being right didn't make what we were about to do any less terrifying.

Jonah started to move to the side of the mound.

Felicia put a hand on his chest. "Richard and I will scout. The rest of you, wait here until we return."

"That's too dangerous, Mom," Blaise said. "Josh and I will go."

Richard said, "Who knows the slave traffickers best?"

"Who has the most sins to atone for?" Felicia added quietly.

"That's in the past," her daughter said.

"Yes, and we accept that, but we also accept that we were part of that chain of hate," Felicia said, gesturing toward the barn.

Richard added, "And being forgiven for sins in the past doesn't change the responsibility we have in the present."

"Wait here. We'll signal if we want you to come forward," Felicia said, leaving her pack on the ground and crouching forward.

Richard swung the pack off his back and followed.

Blaise poked her head around the mound on one side and Jonah did the same on the other, their guns ready to fire. The rest of us sat with our back to the dirt wall protecting us from view.

"They're at the barn," Blaise said, after what felt like forever. "Dad's going toward the front."

I imagined him creeping along the weathered wall, dipping low to avoid the foggy window in the center of the long wall.

On either side of the mound there was a startled shift in posture.

"What is it?" Josh asked, as he watched Blaise.

"They've both gone into the barn," Jonah said, his voice tense. "Felicia in the back and Richard into the front."

Gunfire erupted. Blaise stood and ran toward the barn.

"Wait," Josh called as he ran after her.

A moment later Jonah was sprinting toward the barn and I was doing the same. Eli had retrieved Felicia's and Richard's discarded packs and was running beside me. He threw them down when we reached the wall of the barn.

Blaise disappeared into the barn, Josh followed, and then Jonah. The gunfire increased.

I turned the corner in time to see Felicia climb into the driver's seat of the transport truck. Harvesters shot at her, but none hit her. Richard and Blaise returned fire. Richard shot to kill, and did. Blaise shot to stop and did. Josh climbed onto a motorcycle and sped toward Blaise. He slowed and she hopped on, continuing to fire. There were only two harvesters still firing. But they were well protected behind a stack of rotting firewood. Jonah started the other bike, and he sped toward me and Eli. Eli ran and grabbed the packs as Richard held on to the passenger side of the truck. Felicia drove it from the barn, slowing only so Eli could throw himself and the packs into the back. Jonah pulled me onto the bike, in front of him.

"Can you drive?" he yelled over the noise.

"Yes," I shouted back, latching on to the hand grips, though I had no idea how to drive a motorcycle.

"Throttle, right hand. Left hand lever is the clutch," Jonah yelled over the wind. "Right hand lever is the brake, don't get them confused. Left foot shifts up and down."

The bike jerked forward as I attempted to shift into a higher gear.

"Sorry," I yelled as Jonah's grasp around my waist became so tight it was difficult to breathe. His arm relaxed a little as the bike stopped lurching forward.

Jonah kept his left arm around me and he fired behind us with his right. I followed the truck. I couldn't see Eli, though I was sure he'd made it on. I pulled to the passenger side of the truck. Richard was in, window down, gun pointed behind him. I veered back behind the truck.

We were out of the barn and yard and onto the main dirt road. The guns behind us were silent.

The truck started to slow and I did the same. I felt Jonah take the gun from the back of my waist. He unzipped my pack and slipped it in. He returned his hands to my waist, a pistol in his hand, laying it on my thigh.

Josh and Blaise came beside us.

"You okay?" she yelled as Josh and I moved the bikes closer to one another. Each of us concentrated; driving a motorcycle was more difficult than the movies made it seem.

"Yes," Jonah yelled. "Are there others in the truck?"

"Yes," Blaise shouted. "I don't know how many."

At that moment Eli peered from the truck and was relieved when he saw the four of us. He waved and disappeared into the darkness of the canvas-covered truck.

"I guess Felicia thought it was easier to steal the truck than rescue the slaves some other way," Jonah said over the wind, to me.

"Easier maybe, but more dangerous for sure," I said, feeling angry at her for risking my life and the lives of my friends.

The bikes were so loud, I could barely hear Jonah.

"The harvesters will find us on these things," I shouted. "They're so loud, and the road is open."

"People run from the sound of the harvesters, and other harvesters will think we are with them," he answered.

"What about the ones we left in the barn? Won't they get word to the others?" I asked.

"If they have a radio, but I bet they don't. I bet the only one they had was the one in the truck. If we can keep the vehicles for even a few miles, we'll cut hours out of our journey and spare our bodies."

"As long as we aren't caught," I said, trying not to worry.

Jonah was right. Even a few minutes on the bikes would save us hours of walking. It was worth some level of risk, but I felt like easy prey, out in the open, a caravan of loud vehicles on an empty road in the middle of the day. If it were nighttime, I wouldn't worry as much. We could turn off the headlights and at least not be easily seen. But during the day we could be seen and heard from miles away.

Up ahead, the road went through a wooded area. As we entered it, I relaxed a little. Jonah was still armed and

116

so were Blaise and Richard. Motorcycles were fast and agile. It would be difficult for anyone to hit us with fatal accuracy while we were moving at this speed. As we continued forward, I watched the odometer. With every click of a new mile I reminded myself how fast that had gone by and that my legs were not sore.

I repeated these thoughts as we rode through the middle of the open countryside.

Ten
BRIA

I stopped worrying hours ago, about the same time my butt and back started to hurt. I wasn't used to riding or even sitting for more than a few minutes here and there, certainly not for hours. I had welts on my face and arms from where bugs had smashed against me and my hair was twisted and knotted.

"Why would someone ever choose to ride motorcycles for fun?" I called to Jonah.

I heard him laugh.

His lips were close to my ear, so I heard him say, "It wouldn't be so bad if there was a windshield and softer seats," he said.

"And if we weren't constantly waiting to be shot at," I added.

"That would help," he said with amusement. "It is nice sitting so close to you." His arms tightened around my waist.

"No offense, but the appeal of that wore off a long time ago," I said, almost wishing we could walk.

He chuckled. "None taken. I would happily trade a little space between us for a car windshield."

"How much further do you think we'll go on this thing?" I said.

"What does your fuel gauge say?"

I leaned a bit to allow the headlights from the truck to shine around me. "Empty," I said, wondering how long it had read that way.

"Then, not far on the bike," he joked. "Hopefully, the truck has more fuel."

"How many people do you think are already back there?" I asked.

After Blaise's bike died, she and Josh took over the driving. Josh was brilliant at navigating, and Richard and Felicia didn't know the way.

Richard and Felicia were now in the back with Eli. That transition had taken seconds, and though we hadn't seen anyone else we knew, there were others. If there weren't, we wouldn't have fought for the truck and the bikes.

"I'm not sure," Jonah said.

He didn't want to speculate about those we rescued and neither did I. Every time we glimpsed Eli, he appeared hurried. He made eye contact with me once and his expression was both furious and brokenhearted. It was better not to imagine what he was seeing and who he was helping. It was better to focus on the road and the bike and my physical discomfort. That was easier.

"We're about to find out," I said as the bike slowed and I pulled to the side of the road to avoid being hit by the truck.

Jonah put his leg down to support the bike as I got off and ran to the truck that was now parked a few yards in front of us. It felt good to run. It felt good to not be sitting on that bike.

The engine was still rumbling. I followed Jonah to the back of the truck. The glow of red brake lights made the green army canvas appear brown. When Jonah was halfway in, he offered me his hand. I took it and climbed over the gate. Richard came beside us and hit the side of the truck as a signal for Josh to go.

I stumbled to the bed as the truck lurched forward. The canvas topper would offer protection from the wind and bugs. The flatbed was a welcome change to the motorcycle seat. As my eyes adjusted, I could begin to make out the figures that sat around us. We were nine: five of us, and four rescued slaves—a woman and two men, in their late twenties or early thirties. One had dark skin and the others had light skin. A young boy was lying against Eli's folded leg.

Jonah's arm came down around me. My body leaned close to his, my eyes heavy.

"Is he okay?" Jonah's voice vibrated in his chest as he asked about the boy Eli was comforting.

"Physically, I think so," Eli said with calm outrage.

Felicia and Richard sat across from us, not looking at the slaves, not looking at us. Each of them was staring at the bed of the truck or the back, at the opening.

Eli was watching them. I wondered if he would struggle to forgive them, as I had. It's easy to offer forgiveness to someone whose sin you never felt or saw. He caressed the hair of the slave child who lay sleeping against him.

Now he had seen it.

***

I jerked awake. The truck was silent. Jonah sat up, kissed me on the forehead, and leaped from the back. I stretched, getting my gun and pack, and followed him.

We were on a road with no houses. There were electrical poles, so I assumed houses must be near, just not near enough to see.

Blaise said, "We got as close as we could."

"Where are we?" Jonah asked.

"Close to the Taits's farm," Josh said.

I turned, the wind lightly lifting the ends of my hair.

"That's less than a day from the town," I said, my voice rising with excitement.

Josh nodded. "The fastest way to the town would be to head northwest, but that means we go through the Tait property."

I didn't need to ask about the apprehension I heard in his voice. He was thinking of Hayden and his family, the scavengers we had rescued the Taits from, as well as the men and women they cared for.

"I doubt they're still there," I said.

"We do too, but do we want to risk it?" Blaise asked.

"There are threats everywhere," Jonah said. "At least we know that property. We can avoid the fields and buildings. Even if they're there, they won't be in the woods."

Behind us the truck was emptying. Richard was the first on the ground. Next, a woman in slave clothes, her hair tangled. Two men, also in slave clothes, one with skin so dark it made him hard to see in the night, the other with light skin. Then came Felicia, helping the boy who had been sleeping on Eli. Finally, Eli climbed from the truck. The slave woman's eyes were wide with fear.

"It's okay," Blaise said, "we aren't going to hurt you."

The woman didn't respond.

"We aren't going to hurt any of you," Richard said, his voice severe, as if he was ordering them not to be afraid.

The woman stayed back. The men glanced at one another in an uneasy way and then came toward us slowly.

The man with the light skin shoved the man with the dark skin toward us. He fell onto Jonah. In that instant the light-skinned man sprinted away from us, into a field. We watched him disappear into the night.

"Should we go after him?" Felicia asked.

"Staying or leaving is his choice," Jonah said. "Are you okay?" he asked the man that had fallen against him.

The man looked away and almost cowered at Jonah's question.

"Where is the woman who was here?" Josh asked.

We all turned. She was gone too, running down the road we had just come from.

"They clearly aren't very smart," Richard said. "There was no reason for them to think we were going to hurt them, and yet they run off in the middle of the night with no weapons. How are they going to survive?"

My skin prickled at the condescension in his voice.

"Are you incapable of seeing the world through someone else's mind?" Jonah said in a sharp tone. "Do you think they think as you do? Of course not, because their life has not been your pampered life."

"Pampered? You call this pampered?" Richard said, his arms open, his voice angry. "Before and after the attack, I've worked hard to support my family. To keep them safe."

"And you think that because that man or woman wore the clothes of a slave, they haven't worked hard?" Jonah said.

"Don't put words in his mouth," Felicia said. "He never said that."

Eli stepped forward. "You believe yourself superior to others, Richard, and you're not," he said, his voice calm yet commanding. "No one is superior to anyone else. No one is more valuable than anyone else. Until you fully accept that, you will continue to see those who stumble as worthy of stumbling and those who soar as worthy of soaring. You will tell yourself that it is because of you that you were never a slave, that your wife and daughter are by your side rather than dead or enslaved, because of something you did. You must relinquish this false control and stop allowing pride to dominate you. If you don't, you'll continue to fall in massive ways."

"I'm not a child, to be lectured," Richard replied angrily. "I've gotten out of life what I've put into it."

"Perhaps," Eli said, keeping his voice even. "Though I personally am always a bit fearful that one day I will truly receive from life what I have put into it."

His words were cryptic. Did he believe he deserved something bad? That was impossible. Eli was good; he deserved only good. But if that were the case, why would he say he feared it?

"None of this matters right now," Josh said in frustration. "What matters is we can be seen from miles away in all directions."

"Take us toward the Tait farm," I said. I wanted to get to the town. I wanted to find East and I wanted to go home.

Eli spoke to the boy and the man. "You two are welcome to come with us. We will not force you. We are not your captors. You are free and you can make the choice you want."

"I want to stay with you," the boy said, his voice young and scared. He was no older than five.

"I'm very happy to hear that, Sebastian," Eli said, and extended his hand. Sebastian took it and the two moved forward, following Blaise and Josh, who had started walking—angry at someone, though I wasn't sure if it was us or her parents.

"What about you?" Jonah asked the man who had been a slave.

"Are they in charge?" he asked, nodding toward Richard and Felicia, who had begun walking.

"Officially, no one is in charge," Jonah answered.

"But unofficially, they are definitely not in charge," I added.

He hesitated. "All right," he said.

The three of us began to move forward, following the others.

"What's your name?" I asked.

"Beau," he answered.

"Do you know the boy, Sebastian?" Jonah asked.

In front of us, Sebastian began leaning against Eli as they walked. Eli stopped and lifted Sebastian into his arms. Sebastian flopped onto Eli's shoulder and closed his eyes.

"That boy's seen too much. All of us at that place saw too much," Beau said. "He was with the kids. I never interacted with them."

"Did he have parents?" I asked, my heart breaking at the thought of him being taken from his parents, or worse—the memory of Annalise and her parents lying dead at the harvesters' camp piercing my thoughts.

Beau didn't answer at first. Finally, he said, "Have you been to a slave camp before?"

"Yes," Jonah answered. "It was hell on earth."

The memory made me shiver, and even Jonah's hand in mine could not chase away that fear.

"Yes," Beau said, his body tensing beside us. "No, I don't think that boy had parents. I never saw anyone fighting for him. 'Course, they may have been killed before I got there. I'd only been there a month. Felt like an eternity. He was there before me."

"What about the others in the truck?" I asked. "Did they come from the same place as you two?"

Beau shook his head. "They were captured on the way."

In front of us Eli shifted Sebastian to his other shoulder. Sebastian's head lifted and flopped back onto Eli's shoulder again.

"He must be exhausted," I said as we walked through the darkness toward the Tait property.

After several minutes, Jonah spoke. "The place where they took you from, where was it?"

"Southeast of Chapel Hill," Beau said.

Fear coursed through me and I felt it in Jonah too. That was close to our families, very close. And much closer than we thought the government forces had reached. We thought we'd left our families protected and safe, but we were wrong. And our mistake could cost them their lives.

Trying to keep my voice from shaking, I asked, "What do we do?"

Jonah held my hand. "We tried before to pretend what was happening in DC wouldn't affect our home and families. We were wrong. They are encroaching and they won't stop until we stop them."

He was talking of war. "What about our family? We can't leave them unprepared for a war," I said, wanting to turn around, to go to them and warn them, to fight alongside them, to protect them.

"We're less than a day from the town. We'll go there first and then decide," Jonah said.

It was the logical decision, but not what I wanted to hear. I wanted to hear: We turn around and we fight.

Eleven
EAST

My eyes opened to the first rays of sunlight. My body was sore from the hard bed, yet my mind was clear. I had slept dreamlessly the entire night. It was a gift to be able to sleep where I felt safe.

I swung my feet from the bed and instantly remembered why I forced myself to move past my fear of dogs. They were everywhere in this town.

At the sight of my feet on the dirt floor, two of the young dogs, who were almost as big as their parents, emerged from under the bed. Or at least their paws did. They were stretching, their long claws pushing against my feet. I shivered involuntarily at the feel of their nails against my skin.

"They're saying good morning," Haz said as he folded the blanket he'd slept on and laid it on Thomas's empty bed.

I cautiously stepped from the bed as the dogs wiggled out from underneath and wagged their tails expectantly at me.

"They want you to pet them," Haz said.

"Yeah, and I want a working car," I said to the dogs, and slipped into my shoes.

Haz chuckled to himself. "Do you like cats?" he asked with a quizzical expression.

"Cats hunt the same things I do," I said, with a sort of "do you know me at all" expression on my face.

He shook his head, his dimples so big Blaise would've gushed. "Yeah," he said, "I didn't figure you for a cat person."

"I like practical," I said.

"And pets aren't practical?" Haz asked.

"Most are just more mouths to feed, but some are useful," I answered.

"Like what?" Haz answered, sitting on Thomas's bed.

"Horses. We have two of those. They helped us move from my parents' house to Bria's property. They were pretty essential. My grandmother's chickens are also helpful," I said, stretching. "Where's John?"

"He was up before any of us. He's probably already gathering food so we have no more excuses to delay." Haz stood, following me toward the door of the hut.

"I didn't want to trick him, but I'm thankful for the peaceful sleep," I said as we left the hut. The sun was still low in the sky, barely visible through the trees, but already, most of the townspeople gathered around the morning cooking fire.

Gus handed me a cup of tea as I approached and I gladly accepted it. John was answering questions and explaining to everyone that we would be leaving any minute for Raven Rock and then going to North Carolina to find his daughter and, hopefully, his wife and son afterward.

It was difficult to hear him speak with such hope of finding his wife and son alive. Most of our country's population was dead. His daughter survived by some miracle. Asking that he find his wife and son alive was expecting more than any of us could hope for. Certainly, more than any of the people in this town could.

Momma Pryce stood to one side and came toward Haz and me. When she reached us, she gave me a hug.

"I'm so glad his daughter is alive. That man needs someone to pour his hope into," she said as Haz bent and kissed her on the cheek. She reminded me so much of Nonie.

"Yes, he does, and Juliette needs him too," Haz said.

Momma nodded. "He says you're leaving this morning."

"We can't make him keep waiting. It isn't fair to him or Juliette," I said.

"It certainly isn't," Momma Pryce said. "He's about to jump out of his skin."

In that moment John realized we were there and quickly pushed his way out of the group and came toward us.

"I filled our bottles, and they've given us some smoked meat," John said, handing Haz and me our packs.

The meat was very generous, but I longed for vegetables, real ones grown in a garden, not bitter greens gathered along the way.

As John flung his own pack onto his back in expectation of an immediate departure, I accepted that the next vegetables I ate would be from my mother's garden.

"I'm sorry you're leaving so quickly," Momma Pryce said as she looped her arm through mine.

"It's best we find Jael and Ash, and get John to Juliette," Haz said.

"You say that so easily, Detective, as if every moment when you're out there you won't be risking your life," Momma Pryce said, looping her other arm through his arm and gazing up at him.

She was right. He did say it easily, and so did I. We weren't blind to the risks, but we weren't going to hide from life, either.

"You two are just like my kids, cut from the same cloth, and I'm probably just like your mothers, worried every moment of the day," she said as she leaned her head against Haz's strong shoulder.

"My mom passed away," he said softly.

"Hmm, I wonder if that matters, or if she's still worried," Momma Pryce said, and though she spoke of Haz's mom, she was asking for herself.

"I think she's done being worried," Haz said. "I put her through enough while she was here. She's earned peace."

"I hope you're right, Detective. I hope the worrying ends when this life ends. I've certainly had more than my share. Tell my kids to come home when they're done saving the world," she said, stopping as we reached the trees.

I felt a wave of sadness and pushed it down. I released her arm and gave her a hug. "We love you."

"Be careful, for my sake and your mother's," she said, giving me a hug.

"I promise," I said.

"Will I see you again?" she asked as she held me against her.

I was thankful she could not see my face; I allowed my expression to fall, and lifted it as she released me. I said, "I'm sure you will."

She laughed. "You're not sure of anything and neither am I, but I love you and I'll pray for you. I expect that's all I can do."

I kissed her on a wrinkled cheek. "Goodbye, Momma, I'll do the same for you."

I turned from her and went to stand beside John, while Haz and Momma Pryce said their goodbyes.

I couldn't hear what was said, but Momma kept looking toward me in a way that made me think she was talking about me. Momma was crying after the long hug they shared.

Haz left her side and joined us. "I hate goodbyes," he said as we started down the hill.

"Most people do," I said, not allowing myself to think of Momma, Becca, Gus, and all the others in the town.

As we continued down the hill, I remembered something. "Did she say something about me?" I asked Haz.

He hesitated and then said, "She said you were one of the few women I couldn't scare away."

My face turned red. John angled his body to face us, walking slowly backward. He chuckled as he turned around. "You may not be able to scare her away, but can she scare you away? That's the true test of a man. Is he strong enough to stand beside his woman through it all?"

My face was as red as the reddest berry. His woman? I was not Haz's woman or anyone else's. If Haz had said something that stupid, I would kick his legs out from under him, bringing him to the ground. But John was too weak for that. I'd probably accidentally break his leg and end up having to carry him. So I said nothing.

Haz was smart enough not to respond or make eye contact with either John or me.

As we crossed the field, we startled some birds that flew up from the tall grasses in the distance.

Haz said, "So, your grandma's chickens. Did you like them 'cause they were cute or 'cause you could eat them?"

I paused, remembering our earlier conversation about pets. "Both," I answered, with no hint of amusement, though I felt some.

He laughed loudly, enough to scare five more birds into the sky. "That's what I figured."

I kept my head low, but allowed a smile to form on my lips. Momma Pryce was right. He couldn't scare me away. The problem wasn't him—it was me and the memories that lived inside me.

Twelve
BRIA

We entered the woods near the Tait property as the sun was rising.

"The field is overgrown," Felicia said.

Josh said, "I guess we know the Taits didn't come back here."

"I hope they made it to the town," Blaise said—what we were all thinking.

"Do you think it's safe to go into the field?" Josh asked, undoubtedly excited by the possibility of fresh vegetables.

We focused on the property. The grass had grown to several feet high around the house and barn. There were paths through it, but none big enough for a human to have made.

"Let us go first," Felicia said, indicating Richard and herself, "so we can make sure there's no one in the house or barn."

No one argued. It was the smart thing to do. Send in scouts before we all risked our lives.

"Be careful," Blaise said as her parents started forward.

Jonah lay Sebastian on the ground. He had slept the night in our rotating arms. I knelt beside him as he started to awaken.

"Shh," I said, placing my finger to my lips as Felicia and Richard broke from the safety of the forest and entered the field, staying low to the ground. The weeds and crops were tall enough to block most of their bodies. They followed a game trail to keep the trail they left from standing out to someone glancing out a window. At the house, they stopped, their heads pressed against the wooden sides.

The house was raised, built on concrete blocks or maybe chunks of concrete, it was difficult to tell from a distance. Felicia wasn't tall enough to see into the windows, but Richard was. He peered into window after window, and then together the two climbed onto the porch. Felicia swung the door open. A moment later they returned and began making their way to the barn.

A few minutes after that, Richard signaled for us to come forward. Felicia went back into the barn and returned with the largest wheelbarrow I'd ever seen. No wonder Mr. and Mrs. Tait didn't take it when they fled. It would've been difficult for any of them to have pushed it the day's journey to the town. We were stronger and could take turns.

"Let's salvage what we can," Blaise said as we stepped into the field.

"From the looks of it, the animals around here have been well fed," Josh said, with some discouragement.

He was right. There were tomatoes growing near us that were far from edible; they were either rotten or riddled with bugs or animal bites.

"Those are still good for seed," Blaise said to Josh. "Come with me. Let's find something to put rotten veggies in. Gus will be excited for the added variety of crops."

Josh ran after Blaise. As Richard took the wheelbarrow from Felicia and pushed it toward the field between us and them, Jonah and I stepped into the field, searching for food that could be saved.

"Aren't you going to come?" Eli asked.

I turned. He was speaking to Sebastian. Beau stood off to the side, neither one of them following us or Eli.

Sebastian shook his head. His face showed only fear.

"If he's feeling what I'm feeling, he's not going in there. Seeing this field, it reminds me of where we came from, and I never want to be reminded of that," Beau said, his jaw clenched as he spoke.

"Stay with them," Jonah said to Eli. "There are more than enough of us to fill the wheelbarrow."

"If you follow those trees, we can meet you at the far edge of the property," I said, pointing to the strip of trees we'd hidden in when we first came to the Tait farm.

"For an added bonus, you can see where Sage began falling in love with Hayden, the stellar guy who got her pregnant and left her to die at a harvesters' camp," Jonah said. He was the most outspoken in his disdain for Hayden.

"Lovely," Eli said with a sarcastic edge as he, Beau, and Sebastian began their journey around the field.

"We so should've left Hayden tied to a tree," I mumbled to my husband.

Jonah and I began searching for edible crops, and I said, "I wonder how long it took his family to get untied."

"If he didn't help them," Jonah said, "then, probably at least a day before they could get one of the ropes to break against a tree."

"A day tied to a tree hardly seems long enough for what they did to the Taits," I said.

"No, it doesn't," Jonah said.

"That eggplant is still good," I said, going to it. I tried to pull it from the stalk of the plant, but it wouldn't budge.

Jonah laughed and pulled out his pocketknife. "Mom grew eggplant once. It's like there's a steel cable connecting it to the plant," he said as he cut it loose and handed it to me. I lifted the end of my shirt and created a basket for vegetables.

"There's two more," I said, and Jonah retrieved them.

Ahead of us, Richard and Felicia were beginning to fill the wheelbarrow. We made our way toward them, finding some yellow squash along the way. Both of our shirts were full by the time we got there.

"We're putting the heavier produce in first," Felicia said. She was carrying two medium-sized watermelons to the wheelbarrow. "There's a few more over there that the rats didn't get."

Jonah and I carefully emptied our loads onto the grass beside the wheelbarrow. We each carried two watermelons back to the wheelbarrow. Felicia had stopped harvesting and was now organizing. Richard was carrying some cantaloupes to her. Blaise and Josh returned with plastic grocery bags.

I asked, "What took you so long?"

"We searched the house for anything we could use," Blaise said.

"Find anything?" Jonah asked.

"A few pill bottles, knives, plastic containers we thought seeds could be stored in, and this," Josh said, showing us a ream of printer paper.

"We thought the kids in the town would like it," Blaise said, grinning.

"And then some crayons, because we remembered how much Quinn liked hers. We thought Marjorie's kids might enjoy them," Josh said.

"The kids will love those," I said as Blaise handed the plastic grocery bag with the paper and crayons to her mom.

"We're going to go collect seeds from the plants that have nothing left for us to eat," Blaise said.

She and Josh went through the field, occasionally picking up rotten vegetables from the ground or from a plant.

Jonah and I returned to scouring the field for edible foods. We found several pepper plants that were untouched.

"I wonder if these are the really hot kind and that's why the animals don't like them," I said.

"Maybe. Don't touch your eyes or anything," Jonah said.

After we made a few more trips with our shirts full, Blaise and Josh returned with full bags of rotten vegetables and full shirts of nicely ripened food. Felicia was done loading the watermelons and cantaloupes. She and Richard had begun filling the next layers with eggplants and peppers, and lastly came the beans of different kinds.

"Richard, there was a pitchfork in the barn," Felicia said. "Will you get it? It's a good weapon and a good tool."

Jonah stepped to the wheelbarrow. "I'll push it first," he said.

I never doubted for a moment that he would be first to push it and would end up pushing it far longer than any of the rest of us.

"Anyone want some watermelon?" Blaise asked as she took a watermelon that had been left on the ground and cut into it.

We each bit into large pieces. The sweet juice dripped down my arms and chin. I was sticky but I didn't care. When Jonah finished his piece, Richard had returned, carrying the pitchfork.

We began going toward the trees, Jonah pushing the wheelbarrow, Blaise and Josh carrying bags of smashed vegetables. I carried half a watermelon that we saved for Eli, Sebastian, and Beau.

As we neared the edge of the field, the three of them were there. It was as if they were stuck between two places they didn't want to be. The men were visibly upset, and Sebastian was crying as he clutched Eli's leg.

"You don't need to cry," Felicia said sweetly, kneeling down to be at eye level with Sebastian. "We are all done with the farm, and look, we brought you some watermelon. It's very good and sweet."

I held out the watermelon for Sebastian to see.

"He wasn't crying for you," Beau said.

We glanced at him, but our eyes settled on Eli.

"What's going on?" Jonah asked as he set down the wheelbarrow and Richard and Blaise both readied their weapons.

"I believe we found Hayden's family," Eli said. I spun my head, my back instinctively going against Jonah's as he did the same.

Eli held up his hand. "We are not in danger."

Josh started to protest.

Beau cut him off. "They've been dead a long time."

"Dead?" Blaise said, expressing the same confusion we all felt.

"We found four skeletons tied to trees," Eli said, with a hint of judgment in his voice.

Did he think we killed them? Did he think we should've set them free?

"That's impossible," Jonah said as he left the wheelbarrow and began jogging toward the trees where we had left Hayden's family. Blaise, Josh, Eli, and I followed. Eli pointed them out. They were mostly covered in leaves and plants. I turned away.

I hated death.

"I don't understand," Jonah said. "Even if Hayden didn't help them, they should've been able to break the ropes after a few hours, a few days max."

I heard Jonah step forward and I turned. "Jonah, don't," I said with disgust as he examined the largest of the skeletons that must've been Hayden's dad.

The clothes sat above the bones. Decomposition happens much faster out in the open like this. Even if no larger predators had found the dead bodies, small animals, insects, and bacteria broke down the flesh and muscle within a matter of weeks instead of months.

"Why is there a hole in the chest of that shirt?" Josh asked. "We didn't stab him. Not there, anyway."

"This one is the same," Blaise said. It was the body of Hayden's mom. The shirt was torn and stained brown where it would cover the stomach.

I stepped forward. "We didn't do that."

"Could someone have found them after you left?" Eli asked.

Jonah lifted his head and looked around. "I don't think so. If someone found them, they would've stayed at the property. A few crops were ripe then. Once they realized about the food supply in the field, they never would've left."

"From the inside of the house, it didn't look like anyone has been here, probably, since the Taits left," Blaise said.

"The fields are the same," Jonah said, with a puzzled expression.

"So, who killed these people?" Eli asked.

He was right. They had been killed. I examined the other two bodies. Hayden's sister had multiple puncture wounds in her shirt. Her boyfriend didn't have any, but that just meant that he hadn't been killed in a way that showed three months later.

"Hayden," I said, barely above a whisper.

"Hayden?" Blaise asked.

I locked eyes with Jonah. "Don't you remember when you asked him how he left things with his family, his voice changed. It freaked me out, but I didn't know why. Now I know."

"I do remember that," Jonah said, coming close and wrapping his arms protectively around me. "His tone bothered me too, but I thought I was being too hard on him or judgmental or something."

Jonah's face pressed against my hair. I squeezed him, trying to get rid of the fear I felt.

"Thank God he left her," Josh said as Blaise stumbled into him. His arms wrapped around her.

I held on to Jonah, Josh's words repeating in my head. Thank God Hayden left Sage. I felt so sorry for her before, for having her heart broken, but now I was grateful. So grateful he didn't know where she was or where the others were. He would never find them. Never lose his temper and hurt her. She would never be like Trent and me. No, this was worse. Trent was awful to me, but he never would have hurt his parents. I shivered.

"Are you okay?" Jonah asked.

"Hayden is worse than Trent," I said.

The muscle in Jonah's jaw twitched. He turned to the skeletons and then back to me. "Yes," he said. "Hayden is worse than Trent."

Thirteen
BRIA

Jonah pushed the wheelbarrow, and I carried his pack along with mine. The wheelbarrow wasn't easy to push, though no one would guess that, based on how easy Jonah made it seem. Only when Richard and Josh took over did the pace of the group have to slow so they were not left too far behind. Jonah, by contrast, seemed unfazed by the weight of the overflowing produce he pushed up the last hill that we would climb before reaching Gus's property and the town beyond that. It was barely noon. Thanks to the harvesters' vehicles, a trip that we'd anticipated taking weeks had taken two and a half days.

Since leaving the Tait farm, we spoke few words and almost none by me. Hayden's family had not been good, kind, or giving. That was evident in how they spoke to and of Hayden, and confirmed by what the Taits said of them. Hayden spoke of them being cruel, desiring only to isolate and neglect him. The questions swirling around my mind were: Was he telling the truth, and did it even matter? Was there ever enough misery a person could cause that would warrant being killed by their child, while tied helplessly to a tree? Perhaps Hayden snapped and somehow lost touch with reality. Perhaps he did not understand what he was doing when he plunged the knife through his parents and sister and her boyfriend. Perhaps, but not likely.

He was disturbed, grotesque, and deranged; this was more likely.

Did his family make him that way? They didn't do anything to keep him from becoming the monster he became. Was this simply what they deserved? To be murdered by the child they neglected and mistreated?

I shivered as the thought of Sage and her growing belly entered my mind. I shivered at the thought of what *his* child would become.

"Are you all right?" Jonah asked, beneath the cover of the bright summer leaves.

"Sage is pregnant with his child," I said, feeling my stomach churn as I spoke the words.

Jonah swerved the wheelbarrow around a rock. "And Quinn is the daughter of a rapist."

His words hit me so hard it felt as if I'd hit a tree.

"The child will be beautiful because Sage is beautiful and, like Quinn, Sage's child will be loved and cared for and will grow to be nothing like the creature whose DNA it shares."

"You're right," I said, as if apologizing.

"You don't need to feel bad for thinking that," he said. "I thought the same thing the whole time I was in jail and East was pregnant. I had nothing to do in there but think, so trust me, there's not a thought you can have that I haven't already spent hours agonizing over. But when I held my niece or my sister, everything was fine. She wasn't evil like the man that created her. She was beauty and goodness. Sage's child will be the same."

A warm wind rustled the leaves. The day would be unbearably hot, were it not for the shade of the trees.

"How did we not see him for who he was?" I asked, feeling fear and anger at how trusting we'd been.

"How could we have ever predicted that?"

"Somehow," I said, "we should've known."

He set the wheelbarrow down. His red, raw hands reached out to mine. "You didn't miss a clue and neither did any of the rest of us. Murdering your family like that is a level of evil that only the most deranged can even think of. Their deaths do not rest on our shoulders."

"But we left them tied to those trees," I said.

"Yes, and that saved the Taits and it saved us," Jonah said as he pulled me toward him. "Hayden's family wasn't innocent. They may not have deserved to be killed by their son, but don't forget they were trying to kill us. We didn't harm them and we did not wish them harm." He bent his head to peer into my eyes. "You did this before with Trent. You blamed yourself for his actions. It wasn't true before and it isn't true now."

Jonah's shirt was damp with sweat as I held him. The closeness of his body kept my tears away. I forced myself to accept his words. This was not my fault, just as Trent's killings had not been my fault.

"Thank you, I needed to hear that," I said, reaching up and placing my lips on his.

"That's what I'm here for, to make sure you don't claim ownership of all the world's awful stuff." He brushed my face with the back of his finger. "We have to get going. The others are waiting on us," he said as he placed his hands on the wheelbarrow and started forward.

In front of us the others were sitting on rocks and logs, sipping water from their bottles. Eli was sharing his with Sebastian and Beau.

Eli stood. "Do you want me to take over?" he said to Jonah.

"No, we're almost to the top. I'll let you have it some on the way down."

Jonah was right; the top of this hill was in sight and once we reached the other side, we would be able to see the hill of the town.

"Oh my gosh," Blaise said, eyes wide as she put the cap back on her water bottle.

"What is it?" Josh asked with concern.

"I just realized, what if Hayden hadn't left Sage? What if he was there at the house right now?" She stared, wide-eyed, at Josh and then at me.

"Come on, don't think about him anymore," Josh said, and I was sure they had been having similar conversations as Jonah and I.

"We're close to the town," Josh said, pulling his wife forward. "Let's keep moving."

The rest of us followed in silence, except for Felicia, who would periodically point out plants we could eat and others that were poisonous. I tried to listen whenever we were close enough to her. It's because of the books Blaise took from her mom's library that we were able to so easily survive in the woods.

"We shouldn't have left," Jonah said, interrupting my thoughts about the various ways to prepare dandelions and cattails. "You were right, it was a selfish decision. I wanted to be a hero and save my sister."

"That's not why you wanted to come and you know it. You love East and she's in danger. You wanted to come and bring her home, to make her safe."

"And in the process, I risked not just everyone's life here, but those at home too. Without us they aren't as strong. What if Hayden was there?"

"He's not there, and they did just fine without us the last time we were gone. More than fine, they did great," I said.

"They had Eli," Jonah countered.

"And now they have Sara, Sage, and Juliette."

"Sage is pregnant," Jonah said.

"And not due until March. She can work just as hard as anyone else at this point and, unlike Sara and Eli, she's not averse to violence. In a lot of ways, Sage is better for them to have around than Eli. She's more cunning and not afraid to fight. And Juliette is just as good a shot as Eli and your dad."

"Still, we should be there," Jonah said.

"We will be soon. We'll find East and get home, which is exactly what we're doing," I said.

At that moment the trees ended, and we saw the field in which the house belonging to Gus and his son Thomas once stood. Beyond their open land was the hill our beloved town stood on.

"Think how much quicker the journey here was. Three days ago, we woke up at home. This evening we're already at the town," I said, trying to give Jonah hope. "We'll be home before you know it."

"It will never be soon enough," he said, his expression worried.

Fourteen
EAST

With the sun low in the sky, we stood on a well-paved asphalt road in the middle of a mountain forest. The road was out of place. It was the reason we'd picked this mountain.

"I think we're getting close," I said.

John asked, "Shouldn't we go into the woods?"

He was right. We always avoided roads, but something about this place told me that if we were on the right mountain, it didn't matter if we stood on the road or not—we were being watched.

Haz said, "If Raven Rock is what you and Pam think it is, then no, the woods won't help."

In the distance I could see the gate that made this deserted two-lane road into something very different from all the roads we'd been on before. If John and Pam were right, this was where the actual US government was now headquartered and, I guessed, or more accurately, I hoped it would not be as easily broken into as DC or Camp David.

"Are we sure this is what we want to do?" I asked, feeling a pang of apprehension.

Haz stopped. I could sense his feelings; they were the same as mine. He wasn't afraid, but he was cautious. It was unlikely we would be able to fight our way into or out of this place. We needed to be clear on what to expect. We needed to acknowledge that if we continued on this path, it was entirely possible it would lead to our deaths.

"John should stay here," I said, suddenly aware that if we failed, Juliette's father could be killed.

"Stay here?" John asked in surprise, and I wondered if he had been so focused on getting to Juliette that he forgot the risk of death along the way.

"Juliette has lost enough," Haz said, as if reading my mind. "She needs her father, which means you need to go to her even if we can't. As much as we hope the people through that gate are on our side, our hope doesn't matter."

I stepped toward John. "We don't even know if they'll give us a chance to explain who we are or if they'll shoot on sight." I kept the words separated from my emotions. Now was not the time for me to feel, or the time to risk John's life. He needed to understand that.

John stepped back, his body deflating, the gravity of the situation hitting him. He might be making the journey to his daughter without us, not because he was impatient or we were unwilling to help him, but because we were dead.

"How will I find her?" John asked with hesitation.

He was not someone who was used to backing away to save himself. He was doing it now, only for Juliette.

"Head south until you find the interstate. Stay to the woods, don't walk on the roads," I cautioned.

"I know that," John said in annoyance.

I ignored him; he thought he understood, but he didn't. He hadn't lived in this world long enough to understand. "Keep heading south and hide if you see anyone. Eat worms, if you have to, and drink rainwater collecting on leaves. Don't go near people. Halfway through North Carolina there's a town called Hoodville. Bria's home is there, to the west of the interstate. Juliette will be there waiting for you." I felt a sudden surge of emotion. Quinn would be there waiting for me. I stuffed it aside.

"You'll see the remains of a dirt road in the middle of a falling-down wooden fence. Follow the road to an old stone house. They will be there."

He watched me, taking in every detail I told him. He sensed my pain. The awareness threatened to hold me back, to keep me from doing what I came here to do.

John hesitated. "I can go a bit further with you."

Haz shook his head. "You shouldn't have come this far. That was a mistake, my mistake."

"Tell my family I love them," I said, fighting hard to suppress the emotion behind the words.

I started forward, around the corner that led to the gate.

Haz followed. John stayed hidden, watching us as we walked toward the closed gate in the middle of the razor-wire fence. The gate was rolled closed. The fence encircled the mountain. I wondered for a moment if it, like Camp David's, was electric. As the hum of electricity filled the air I stopped wondering. We were close enough now to see the tiny guard shack, which was unmanned. There were several cameras.

"Do you think they work?" I asked.

"If that fence works, so do the cameras," Haz said, his low voice indicating he thought the microphones also worked.

Behind us, twigs snapped. My face flushed with anger. John was following us, keeping to the woods. I didn't dare tell him to run. If they were watching us, they would see my signal to him and know where he was, though they probably already did.

My hand tightened on my gun as I detected movement inside the guardhouse. Haz did the same as the door swung open and soldiers stood before us, the gate separating us. Their guns pointed at us. We stopped.

This was why we were here, I reminded myself. To face what there was to face and learn what there was to learn.

More troops came from the guardhouse.

"Where are they coming from?" I asked. The building was too small to house even three of them, let alone the dozen that now stood, weapons pointed, in front of us.

"Underground," Haz responded.

Of course, this entire complex was underground. I fought the urge to look at my feet. I felt as if I was standing on an anthill.

"Drop your weapons," a voice boomed as one of the soldiers stepped slightly forward, the gate still closed between us.

They were wise not to open it until they were sure we could do no damage.

I shifted my eyes, not moving my head, so I could see Haz. He was doing the same. Our eyes connected and turned back to the soldiers in front of us. Haz began to lower his body to the ground. I copied his movements.

A loud *bang* came from the guardhouse. Reflexively I jerked upright, pointing my weapon at the figure moving swiftly from the building.

"Lower your weapons," the figure commanded.

Joy filled me as the figure with short spiky hair came into view.

"Jael!" I said, as the scene before me changed.

The soldiers lowered their guns, and the gate rolled open. We ran to each other. Haz followed at a cautious speed.

"Sorry about that," Jael said. "Ash was supposed to be watching the gate cameras, but he was goofing off."

I held her close, relief washing over me. She was alive and had enough power to tell the others to put down their weapons. We would not die today.

"Man, it's good to see you," Haz said, putting his arms around both of us and lifting us slightly off the ground.

"You're stronger than you look, Detective," Jael said as she wiggled free from his arms.

"Sorry about that," Haz said, realizing the hug had made her uncomfortable. "Were you expecting us?"

"We saw you leave DC and figured it was only a matter of time before you came here," she said. "We wanted to avoid the gunpoint reception that we clearly failed to avoid."

"You saw us leave DC?" I asked.

Jael cocked her head to the side. "We were right. About the whole thing, we were right."

My heart beat faster. The government—the real government survived and it was beneath my feet.

Fifteen
BRIA

As we stepped onto the hill I was overcome with fear—fear that the town had fallen and our friends were not there. It had been months since we were last here; anything could've happened in that time. What if Trent's commander returned and demanded their allegiance? Was this town now a government-sanctioned settlement? Would they capture me and hand me over to the commander as the woman who murdered his lieutenant? No, I decided, as long as our friends there were alive, that would not happen.

My fears calmed as Honeybee, Jasper, and their puppies, which were almost full-grown, ran toward us.

Behind them came their owners: Gus, his son Thomas, and some of the other children from town.

"Someone must've been watching to know it was us," Josh said as he began to play with Jasper. Josh bounced from side to side as the dog growled and wagged his tail.

"You're almost as big as your sister Astrea," Blaise said to one of the puppies as she petted its ears.

As happy as I was to see the dogs and the humans that soon followed, I was saddened too. East and Haz were not with them. Neither were Jael and Ash. If any of them were in the town, they would've come to us. I had no hope of seeing them up above where the rest of the townspeople were. Jonah must've felt like me, though he kept his expression joyful. I did my best to do the same.

James Tait was one of the first people we spotted when we reached the top of the hill, and at the sight of him I did not have to force a feeling of joy. It poured forth, filling the world around me. He was there, and safe, and that meant his family would be as well. The Taits, who we rescued from Hayden's family, had made it safely to our town.

"Hey, James, tell your mom we brought her harvest," Josh called out happily.

As we entered the town we were immediately surrounded by dozens of friends. It felt good to be with them, to know they were okay. From the back of the crowd I saw Mrs. Pryce and Becca.

"My crops!" Mrs. Tait yelled as she rushed toward us. "And our rescuers!" she said as she hugged Blaise.

"Did you make it here all right?" Blaise asked her.

"Yes, no trouble at all," Mrs. Tait answered.

"The walk wasn't bad. Less than a day, like you said," Mr. Tait said, shaking Josh's hand.

"What was our house like? Were those bad people still there?" Simon, one of the men the Taits took care of, asked.

I put my hand in Jonah's. Simon was so good and innocent; Hayden's family had treated him cruelly, but even so he would not understand Hayden's actions.

"Your house was just as you left it," Blaise said, not answering the question about the others.

Mr. and Mrs. Tait recognized the omission, but those they took care of did not.

"I'm Eli, Jonah and East's big brother," Eli said, purposely interrupting the conversation.

"Hi, Eli. I'm Simon."

"Nice to meet you, Simon," Eli said, shaking his hand.

"And we are Blaise's parents," Felicia said as Mrs. Pryce and Becca approached. "Our names are Felicia and Richard."

"You found them?" Mrs. Pryce said with wonder.

"We did," Blaise said, giving her a hug.

"And this is Sebastian and Beau," Eli added. "We happened to meet them along the way."

"We were slaves, and they freed us," Beau said, correcting him.

Mrs. Pryce's face flashed with anger as it always did when cruelty was mentioned, and then it softened. "We're glad you're both here."

Marjorie stepped forward. Her youngest had grown but was still strapped against her chest, as he was the first time I saw her. On that visit to the town I watched her two older children paint houses with mud.

She bent down to be eye level with Sebastian. "Sebastian, honey, I was about to feed my children a snack. Would you like to join us?"

Sebastian hesitated. Eli bent down and spoke to him. "My brother says this is a good place, with kind people. Did you see all the children running and playing?"

Sebastian nodded.

"They aren't scared or sad. They are having fun and they have plenty of food to eat."

Marjorie held her hand out for him. The young toddler on her chest giggled at the new boy in town. "Come with us, Sebastian. You are the perfect age to play with my two big kids. My son Jackson would love another little boy around to play tag with and catch bugs. Do you like to catch bugs?"

Sebastian shook his head no.

Marjorie laughed a delicate laugh filled with the love of a mother. "I don't blame you a bit. I don't like to catch them either. Come along and have a snack," she said, placing her hand on Sebastian's back. "Your friends will be right here. They aren't going anywhere."

Sebastian looked up at Eli. The late afternoon sunlight filtered through the leaves, creating spots of light and dark on his young scared face.

"She's right," Eli said, holding Sebastian against his leg. "I'll be right here. You go and have a snack. I'll be watching you, okay?"

Sebastian hesitated.

"It's okay," Eli said, kindly kissing Sebastian on the top of his black hair. "You're safe now. No one is going to hurt you."

Sebastian hesitantly stepped forward. Marjorie took his hand in hers and together they went slowly toward her two older children.

"That woman has such a heart for children," Mrs. Pryce said. "She'll treat him just like her own."

"Yes, I can sense that," Eli said, gazing at Mrs. Pryce the way an old friend would. They were kindred souls and it was evident both of them sensed it.

Jonah asked, "Where are they?"

Mrs. Pryce allowed her smile to fade. "It's nice to see you too, Jonah," Mrs. Pryce said, putting his impatience in check. "And is that a ring I see on your left hand?"

I clasped Jonah's hand with both of mine. "We got married," I blurted out.

"Congratulations!" Becca said, giving me a hug.

Gus stuck his hand out for Jonah. "You got a good one," he said as he and Jonah shook hands.

"Yes, sir," Jonah said. "The very best."

"That's good," Mrs. Pryce said. "Very good. Marriage is beautiful when it's done right, and I can tell you two are doing it right."

"We're trying," I said, leaning against Jonah.

"That's the key, both of you trying," Mrs. Pryce said.

"Ain't that the truth!" Josh exclaimed. "I'm always telling this one, try harder," he joked, poking at Blaise who, if she had a fault, it was that she tried too hard at life.

She wrapped her arms around his waist. "I can't imagine anyone in the world making me laugh as much as you do," she said, kissing him playfully.

"That's the other key," Mr. Tait said. "Laughing."

"As much and as often as you can," Mrs. Tait said, giggling at how silly Josh and Blaise were acting.

Laughter was not something Jonah and I had an abundance of. Maybe someday when we were home and safe and life was easier, maybe then we would laugh more.

"Is my sister here?" Eli asked.

He also needed more laughter in his life, I decided.

"You just missed her," Gus said. "She and Haz were here this morning."

My eyes grew wide with hope. We were so close.

"They went to Raven Rock," Becca said.

"Raven Rock?" Richard repeated.

Mrs. Pryce nodded. "Do you know about it? Most of us here didn't."

"Maybe he was in the military or a politician," Gus said. "Your kids knew about it and so did the politicians they were with."

Richard shook his head. "I enjoyed reading about the history of our country, but I was never in the military and definitely never in politics. Why did they go there?"

"What is it?" Beau asked.

"A government bunker inside the mountains of Pennsylvania," Richard said. "Not far from here, if I had to guess."

"Yep. As it turns out, it's mighty close. Who knew?" Gus said, and I remembered that he'd spent his whole life on the farm that led to this town.

"After you all left, East and Haz went with Jael and Ash and another man named Seth, to Camp David," Mrs. Pryce said. "They freed three prisoners, all politicians."

"One of those prisoners never made it back," Gus said, arms folded.

"I'm sorry," Felicia said.

"He didn't die—at least we don't think he did," Gus said. "Him and that guy Seth were together, and from what we know of the two of them, they were the worst two to put together."

"Why?" Jonah asked.

After a pause, Mrs. Pryce said, "They both struggle with doing what's right."

Gus said, "The politician they rescued, his name is Derrick. Apparently, he was part of blowing up the world."

We all stared at him.

I said, "H-he created … the light?"

Mrs. Pryce said, "He did not create it, but from what the other two from Camp David said—John and Pam are their names—he was one of the main facilitators."

My knees buckled. Jonah put an arm around me to steady me.

My mind was spinning. Somehow, knowing the name of someone who did this made it that much worse. Like all the destruction and deaths were personal attacks.

"Why did East save him?" Blaise asked, her tone sounding ashamed and disgusted.

"They didn't know who they were saving," Becca said, defending them. "And John and Pam, the other two they saved, were innocent, so it's good they helped them."

"Who is Seth and why was he with my sister, if he couldn't be trusted?" Jonah asked, grasping, trying to make sense of something that was senseless.

"He followed us here," Mr. Tait said.

"You don't know that," Mrs. Tait said to her husband.

"Someone was following us, and mercifully, we made it here before they had a chance to ambush us," Mr. Tait said. "Then Seth shows up a few hours afterward. He was following us."

"We don't know he was going to ambush us," Mrs. Tait said.

Her husband raised an eyebrow at her.

"It's likely," Mrs. Tait acknowledged, "but we don't know for a fact."

"He was going to ambush you and your kids, and you let him go with my sister?" Jonah asked, with an edge of anger to his voice.

"She wanted him there," Gus said. "Don't get me wrong. She didn't like him or trust him any more than the rest of us, but you know how she is. Her, Haz, Jael, and Ash are all the same, always putting themselves last. They needed to go, and they didn't want to leave Seth here with us if they weren't around to keep an eye on him."

"They said that?" Josh asked.

"Of course they didn't say that!" Gus exclaimed in amusement. "That would be admitting way too much about how softhearted they all are. It wasn't hard to figure out. Your sister isn't good at pretending she likes someone when she doesn't."

Jonah offered a slight smile and said, "She's never been good at that."

"It's a good thing," Gus said. "You know where you stand with that one."

"She's like my kids, selfless to a flaw, and Haz is the same," Mrs. Pryce said, as if she was both proud and fearful of their selflessness.

I supposed she was. She raised Jael and Ash to be amazing people, but that quality never ceased to put them in danger.

Josh said, "We've been gone three months, and they left only this morning to go to Raven Rock?"

Mrs. Pryce said, "My kids took Pam to Raven Rock weeks ago, and East and Haz took John to DC."

"DC?" Jonah said with concern.

"But they made it back," I said, reminding him before he could worry.

"Yes, they arrived late last night and left at first light for Raven Rock," Gus said.

"It turns out Juliette is John's daughter," Becca said, excitedly rocking onto her tiptoes.

"Juliette?" Blaise said. "Our Juliette?"

"Juliette's dad is alive?" Eli asked. He seemed to want to sit down, but there was no log or bench beside him, so he grabbed onto my arm instead.

Becca grinned, bounced, and nodded at the same time.

"That's incredible," Richard said.

"A miracle," Eli responded.

"A miracle indeed," Mrs. Pryce said.

Josh's face held a puzzled expression. "So, John is Juliette's dad, and they took him to Raven Rock?" he asked. "Why didn't they bring him to us? It could have saved us a trip." He said the last part under his breath, though several of the people heard and laughed.

Mr. Tait said, "East and Haz promised they would take John to Juliette, but first they wanted to share what they learned in DC with Jael and Ash."

Puzzled, we looked at him.

"Pam and John have this theory that the government in charge of DC isn't really the government," Becca said. "And that the real government is lying low in Raven Rock and potentially other government bunkers across the country."

"Not the real government?" Richard said, stumbling to a bench a few feet from him.

He was asking a question, but in a way that made me believe he already knew the answer.

Felicia slumped down beside him. "Not the real government," she repeated, the two staring at each other.

"What do you mean, it isn't really the government?" Blaise asked. Her focus shifted from Becca to her parents and back again.

"That's what Pam and John thought," Becca said. "They didn't think the government would do the things that've been done."

"The government's not that great. Why wouldn't they kill people?" Blaise asked.

"They never said it was great," Mrs. Tait replied. "They never defended it at all. They just thought that the government would not be doing things the way they're being done."

"Like what?" Beau asked, his eyebrows pulled together in focus.

Gus spoke up. "The day after the attack, all the politicians in DC were rounded up and taken to Camp David. John and Pam were two of 'em. Pam's husband was shot when he tried to save her, and John was pulled from his family."

Josh said, "Why were they rounded up? Did someone think they had something to do with the attack?"

"No. That's the thing," Becca said. "All they could figure out was that they were seen as a threat."

"That makes no sense," I said.

"Exactly," Gus responded. "It makes no sense that the government should be threatened by a few politicians. What difference could they make, what harm could they do? If anything, the government—the real one—would want to tap them to help since they were already elected and all that."

"But that's not what happened," Becca said. "John and Pam said all the others were killed except the three of them."

"There was no reason to fear them, unless you had no right to the power you were trying to take," Gus said.

There was silence until Jonah spoke. "What do you two think?" He was watching Richard and Felicia.

Richard closed his eyes.

"That could be true," Felicia said. The words seemed difficult for her to say.

I wondered if she and Richard had justified the murders they committed as somehow necessary to the survival of our nation. If those they murdered for were actually working against our nation, then even that excuse was now gone.

Richard raised his head to reply. "At the time, it never occurred to us that those driving military trucks and wearing military uniforms would not be part of the military, but now …"—he lowered his head and rubbed both his hands through his hair—"it's like a lightbulb going off in my mind. All these small instances that at the time meant nothing, but now—now they mean everything," Richard said, as if he felt sick.

Blaise stepped toward her parents. "What sort of instances?"

175

"It was always the same truck and the same people," Richard said. "Surely, the government had more than one truck and a few officers."

"We drove a different truck here," I said.

"And the slaves," Felicia said, ignoring my comment. "Would our government ever use slaves?"

"It did before," Beau said in anger.

"But would it do it again?" Richard asked, ignoring the anger in his words. "Would it really stoop that low, even in a time of crisis?"

"You did," Josh said, his words biting.

"Yes," Richard said, keeping his voice even. "We did, but our failure wasn't thought out or planned. Theirs was. It wasn't a slope they gradually slid down. They were there at the bottom of it from the first time we met the soldiers, or whoever they were."

"It's not just that," Felicia said, intently focused on her husband.

"No," Richard said. "There were a myriad of tiny transgressions that, like I said, at the time seemed like nothing, but now seem like everything."

He stared at his wife and she stared back, the lies they believed crumbling around them.

"What were they hoping to do by going to Raven Rock?" Jonah asked, turning his attention away from Richard and Felicia.

"Jael and Ash wanted to get Pam to Raven Rock and somehow save the world," Becca said, only half joking.

Mrs. Pryce said, "Pam believed Derrick when he told her that if he could get to Raven Rock, he could make things right. She believed that and for that reason believed she, too, could make a difference. Jael and Ash agreed to help her. John also believed it, but he wanted to try to find his family first. Haz and East volunteered to take him to DC, the place where he last saw them."

Jonah said, "Now East, Haz, and John have gone to Raven Rock?"

The others nodded.

"We need to go," Jonah said impulsively.

"The sun is about to set and it's not a full moon," I said softly. "We should stay here for the night."

Jonah looked from me to Blaise and Josh. They must have held the same expression I did.

"Is it all right if we stay for the night?" Jonah asked, turning to Mrs. Pryce.

"You never need to ask that," Mrs. Pryce said. "You are always welcome."

Sixteen
EAST

A tall soldier stepped forward. "There's another one about fifty yards that way," he said, pointing to the trees where John was hiding.

"That's John. He's a friend," Haz said to the soldier.

"Signal for him to come out," the soldier said. "We need to lay eyes on him before we can return to base."

Haz turned and waved to John. John emerged from the trees slowly, cautiously stepping onto the road and coming toward us.

"Pam's going to be happy he's here," Jael said.

The soldier cleared his throat.

"Right," Jael said. "Madam President, not Pam. I keep forgetting that."

"President?" Haz asked, raising his eyebrows.

"The president was shot a few weeks after the vice-president. All the others who were in line are either dead or haven't made it to Raven Rock," Jael said.

"Have they been sitting here waiting for someone in line for the presidency to show up?" Haz asked.

"That's the way it works," Jael said. "Ideally, the Secret Service would've brought them here, but there aren't many of them left. Those more directly in line knew it and knew to come here. Since they haven't arrived, it's assumed they're dead. Pam became the default president, something Derrick claimed to be aware of."

"Is Derrick here?" I asked, my fists involuntarily clenching at the thought of the man we helped escape, the man who helped destroy the world.

"He and Seth, the coward, are both here," Jael said in a biting tone. "Pam's first act as president was to have them locked up. She's since released Seth. She wanted him escorted from the base, but when we told her we thought he'd try to take from others, she decided to allow him to stay on and work for food. He seems content to not have to hunt for food. He's not allowed access to weapons or knowledge, so hopefully he's not a threat."

"What Derrick did was treason at the highest level," John said. "Why has she allowed him to live?"

Jael shrugged. Clearly, Derrick's life meant little to her. "Pam said enough lives had been lost, but to be honest, I don't think it's out of the question. She's just too busy right now to deal with it. Plus, I think she might feel like she owes him something," Jael said.

"Owes him something?" John said in disgust.

"He says he's the reason she wasn't killed at Camp David. Said he figured that with so many others dead, the next in line for president would be unclear and he thought it could be her. He said that was why he fought so hard to keep her alive at Camp David. Of course, he told her that as he was begging her not to kill him, so who knows what's true."

Eli and my dad would agree with Pam that enough lives had been lost. If I was in her position … I doubted I could be like them.

The tall soldier acknowledged us as we entered the gate. "Are you expecting anyone else?"

"No," I replied, following him toward the guardhouse.

He turned to face me. "What's your name?" he asked, his teeth gleaming white beneath his clean-shaven face.

"East," I answered without hesitation.

"That's an unusual name," he said kindly, stepping to the side to allow others to pass.

From behind me, Jael said, "She's an unusual woman, Luke. Now, get going."

Luke winked at her and entered the guardhouse.

"Come on," Jael said, pushing me forward. "No need for Haz to get into a fight before he even enters the base." She said this in a teasing tone, plenty loud for both Haz and Luke to hear.

My face flushed and I said under my breath to her, "Haz isn't like that."

"Flirt with the woman he loves and he'll become like that," Jael answered.

I laughed at the thought of Luke flirting with me and of Haz being jealous, but mostly I laughed in relief that Jael was beside me, leading me not to danger but to safety.

The gate rolled closed, the rest of the soldiers filing in behind us. Inside the tiny building a door that I would've thought was a closet was open. Above us an electric light glowed in the shadow of the ceiling.

"They have lights," I said, though I shouldn't have been surprised, since they had cameras and an electrified fence.

"Wait till you see the base," Jael said.

We climbed down the well-lit stairs, into a tunnel that was wider than a two-lane street. Soldiers filled two jeeps. Engines turned over and headlights flicked on.

"Can I give you a ride?" Luke called out to me. He was sitting in the driver's seat of a third jeep, empty except for him.

Jael shoved herself in front of me. "Have you never seen a beautiful woman before?" she said to him in mock irritation as she climbed into the passenger seat beside him.

John and I each got into the back of the jeep.

"Of course I have," Luke said. "I've seen you, haven't I?" He winked at Jael and started the ignition.

She laughed. "If I didn't know East, I might worry your charm would win her over. As it is … go ahead and try."

"I'm not a bad guy," he said to her, though loud enough for John and me to hear.

Jael said, "But you're not extraordinary, and she deserves extraordinary."

Their conversation should have made me uncomfortable, but the truth was it didn't affect me. I wasn't interested in Luke, so what he did or didn't do made little difference to me. I wasn't sure if I deserved extraordinary, but I wasn't interested in a typical guy and Luke was a typical guy. There was nothing wrong with that; it just wasn't enough to hold or even capture my interest.

As Luke released the brake, the jeep shifted forward, and Haz jumped in beside me. I sensed his arrival and had already moved to the cramped middle seat.

"I wondered when you'd be joining us," Jael said with a smirk.

"I was checking out the tunnel," Haz said. If he was bothered by Luke's attempts at flirting with me, he didn't show it.

We started forward. The tunnel was at least a mile, maybe longer, gradually rising as we continued forward. Either side of the tunnel was lined with Humvees, armored vehicles, trucks, and even small tanks.

"Do these work?" I asked.

"Every single one," Jael answered proudly.

I felt the same pride. There were more working vehicles here than I'd seen in the last nine months, and all but the jeeps we rode in were ready for combat.

At the end of the tunnel the incline increased, and what remained of daylight filtered into the tunnel through the massive doors that stood open. Luke followed the other jeeps out onto a road that appeared no different from any other road. The jeeps came to a stop, and Jael got out. Haz, John, and I did the same.

"Until next time," Luke said, winking at me.

"Ignore him," Jael told me. "He's been cooped up in the base too long. Come to think of it, most of them have been and most are men. Haz, don't let her out of your sight," Jael said, teasing Haz, who pretended not to hear her.

I wasn't wrong. Haz wasn't the type to fight for me; he knew I could do that myself. Though he was definitely the type to fight alongside of me.

"What about you?" I asked Jael, "have they been flirting with you?"

"I've made it clear my husband is the jealous type and he's not above a haunting," she joked, but it revealed the truth. She loved Isaiah deeply and was not ready to allow another into her heart.

How different she and I were. Her heart was filled with love and so was not ready to accept another. Mine was filled with fear and hatred of my past. The result was the same.

The jeeps disappeared back into the tunnel we'd come from. The area around us was sparse, an empty road surrounded by trees with resident birds and squirrels. The sight of squirrels running up and down trees made me pause; it was a common sight before, but rare now. Now where there were people, the squirrels were hunted. These squirrels weren't afraid of humans; they lived in peace with people and were hunted only by their natural predators.

"Do they have food in the base?" I asked.

"Enough to support over three hundred for a decade," Jael said, with a hint of pride.

Our government, her military, had not been as ill-prepared as we had believed.

The soldiers stood near the entrance to the base, though from the outside it looked like nothing more than a rolled-down door to an oversized garage built into a mountaintop. I imagined cameras scanning the area. I stood between Haz and John as the door opened with surprising speed. Regardless of how it appeared from the outside, this was not the entrance to an oversized garage; this was the entrance to a secret military compound, one built specifically to survive an event of an apocalyptic nature.

Armed guards stood at attention as we followed the soldiers. The three jeep drivers, including Luke, jogged behind us to catch up. The doors of the base closed behind them. The noise of the closing doors startled me. It didn't sound like the thin aluminum sheets they appeared to be on the outside. That's when I realized there were two sets of doors. The outside was the rolled aluminum and the inside, thick steel doors that connected in the middle, like the doors of an ancient fortress.

The ground beneath us was rock with poured concrete on top to help smooth the surface. The tunnel here was large enough for a small vehicle like a jeep to drive through. The walls around us and above us were the same, though without the concrete to smooth them out. There was no shortage of electric lights, all of them bright.

As we walked, we went deeper into the mountain, the ground gradually sloping down. We encountered only a few guards. All of them and all of the soldiers with us were armed. Haz and I had been allowed to keep our weapons, though that was only because Pam had already cleared us to do so.

Jael stopped in front of an elevator, which opened. She and some of the others entered. I inhaled and exhaled. Elevators terrified me—one of those childhood fears that I hadn't outgrown. Probably because even now, I would sometimes dream of falling to my death in an elevator.

"You all right?" Haz whispered.

I nodded and stepped forward. I faced the closing door, biting the inside of my mouth, trying to focus on that pain instead of the feeling of being closed into a sealed metal cage plummeting into the depths of the earth.

I fought the panic as we descended so quickly that my ears filled with pressure, a discomfort I used to feel only on planes. The doors opened, and I rushed out and to the side to catch my breath as the soldiers filed past me.

"You don't care for elevators, do you?" John said kindly.

"They're not my favorite," I said meekly, trying to settle my racing mind and churning stomach.

Ash appeared beside us and put an arm around his foster-sister. "Dogs and elevators. What else is the mighty warrior afraid of?" he teased.

"Nice of you to finally show up," Jael said, shrugging off his arm.

"Sorry about that, but it's not like I wasn't working. I just wasn't watching the gate," Ash said.

"Whatever," Jael said, leading us down another well-lit corridor. This one appeared more finished, though the walls were still made only of stone. To our left was a doorframe and a closed metal door.

"Pam's in here, waiting for you," Ash said as he opened the door.

It was a spacious room with a conference table on one end and several elevated screens and several more computers with soldiers sitting at them, at the other end. Pam stood from her place at the table and came toward us.

"I'm so glad you're here!" she said, hugging John and then me.

"Madam President," Haz said respectfully.

"I never wanted this role," she said to the three of us, though addressing John.

"Which is why you're the perfect person to have it," he said.

"The task is overwhelming," she said, as if confiding a secret rather than stating the obvious.

She was not used to admitting when things were too much for her; I could sense that.

John took her right arm in his. "Could there be a better way to spend a life than rebuilding the greatest nation on earth?" he said.

The room was silent as each of us in turn thought about his words. I wanted to go home and hold Quinn and my parents, but John was right. Rebuilding the nation, that was a life well spent. The thought made chills run through my body as I was struck with the truth—that was how I wanted to spend my life. Giving everything to a cause that was something so much bigger than me, that even my fullest contribution would be like the smallest drop in the largest of oceans.

Haz's voice broke the silence. "Is that DC?"

I followed his stare to the screens lining the wall. I hadn't noticed what was on them. I stared harder, trying to understand what I was seeing.

"Yes," Pam answered plainly.

"The others are New York, Philadelphia, Atlanta, Jacksonville, Kansas City, Denver, Dallas, Los Angeles, Las Vegas, and Seattle," Ash added as the images on various screens flipped to different scenes of major US cities.

"There are four cameras in each city," Jael said. "It's how we saw you leave DC."

I continued to stare, my mouth falling open. I closed it. The scenes in front of me showed the structural outlines of those cities, but on the ground the scenes were of destruction, war, and death.

"Is that Beijing?" John asked, stepping toward another screen on a different wall.

My eyes saw but I was unable to understand what I was looking at. There were buildings and statues, both with an architecture that was distinctly foreign. But this was not the part I couldn't understand. I stepped closer to the screen, Haz and John both doing the same.

"Are those bodies?" I asked, my voice unsteady.

"It's Tiananmen Square," Pam said somberly. "This is our only camera in Beijing. Our best guess is they are using this for a staging area for cremation or burial."

"The bodies are out in the open," I said with disgust.

"Beijing's population was over twenty-one million people. In a city made of concrete. Where else should they place their dead?" Pam said.

I said nothing; the truth of my judgment hit me. I was criticizing the Chinese for the way they chose to deal with the tragedy inflicted on them by my nation.

A dozen other screens surrounded this screen. All of them showed major cities across the world. None of the others had turned into mass graves. All of them had been devastated. They looked like war zones or abandoned cities, none of them like the capitals of great nations. I felt the sour taste of bile in my mouth as I watched, acutely aware that we—my great nation and I—had done this.

Seventeen
EAST

I fell into a chair at the long conference table. My feet were sore from the walk here and my mind overwhelmed by the horrific scenes in front of me. John sat on one side and Haz on the other. None of us spoke.

It was worse than I'd imagined, so much worse.

"These are only scenes in the cities," Jael said, sitting across from me. "Everything's always worse in the cities."

I nodded my head and looked at my nails. They were stained with dirt; they never used to be like that. I used to have clean hands and nails. I showered every day. Even as a kid, being clean was always important to me. Now I accepted that dirt would always be under my fingernails. Perhaps death was the same. Before, we hid from death as best we could, and now it was in our faces every moment of every day. When Eli was in the seminary, he told me some saints used to keep human skulls on their desk to remind them of their own mortality. That image never left me and always disgusted me. I picked at my thumbnail and wondered what the saints would think of the destruction before us.

Pam sat beside Jael. "Don't lose hope," she said. "We can't undo what's happened, but we can move forward."

"With a third of the world's previous population," John said, his voice morose, capturing my feelings.

Ash said, "The statistician here thinks it's probably closer to one fourth."

"If you're trying to be helpful, you're failing," I said, glaring at him.

Pam spoke. "One of the scenes in Jacksonville shows a colony along the St. Johns River. For the most part, it's peaceful. Children are growing, the elderly are surviving. And the town Jael and Ash helped establish, we all witnessed how well it is functioning. There will be pockets like that throughout our nation. We simply don't have cameras there. We do, however, have satellites and we've begun using them to view the rural areas. There are pockets of peace everywhere. We simply aren't watching them every moment of the day."

"How are these cameras working?" Haz asked, with a hint of anger that I was sure only I heard.

"Our government was much more prepared than we realized," Pam said, answering Haz's question but speaking to John. "The cameras are inlaid with Faraday cages and their signals are transmitted to satellites high enough above the earth not to be damaged by the explosion."

"So, the people here have been watching the world destroy itself from the comfort of a cave?" Haz asked, his anger now fully present.

"They were prepared, but still caught off guard. Derrick and the others made sure of that," Pam said, as if spitting his name. "All of the workers here have done the best they could and all have lost loved ones," she said with a tone meant to check his righteous indignation.

"The team stationed here was here only to support the base," Jael said. "Their orders were to wait until someone in line for the presidency arrived before doing anything."

Pam began again. "Ordinarily, those in line would've been brought here from all over the country, when the detection systems indicated there was an incoming attack. Because those involved in this attack understood that system and wanted it to fail, it did. Those in charge of the continuity of government had no lead time. All those not involved in the attack were caught just as off guard as all the rest of us."

"It's been nine months," Haz said. "In all that time, no one thought that maybe they should move beyond the safety of this base and help the rest of us?"

"It wasn't business as usual after the attacks," Ash said. "It's taken them months to get communications systems and video feeds back online."

"And they're soldiers," Jael said. "They follow orders. And orders stated they wait for the president."

It made sense to her because she was a soldier; she was obedient to an authority greater than herself. I was not, though in so many ways I envied that about her and Eli. His allegiance was to the authority of the church. When I was younger, the thought of entering religious life entered my mind and just as quickly exited. I could never be obedient. I tried always to do what God asked me to do and follow the teachings set forth by the church, but I was stubborn and oppositional. Those traits were innate, obedience was not.

"DC is not far from here and it is at war with itself," John said indignantly.

"It's always been at war with itself," Ash said, with an almost smile.

Haz was not amused and neither was I.

Fighting the urge to stand and walk out, I said, "How could they sit here and watch while the world burned!"

"It's true the government has survived because of this place and a few others like it throughout the country, but it has survived in an extremely weakened state," Pam said, attempting to bring peace. "The result is a need to be prudent. Where we once intervened in conflicts throughout the world, we would now find it difficult to contain the conflicts in even one of our major cities. Yes, we could do it, but it wouldn't be easy."

"Instead you've chosen to do nothing?" Haz asked. "To allow the factions to kill each other out."

"Raven Rock and other places like this one were not created to protect the people, they were created to protect the nation," Jael said.

"The point of the nation is her people," John said in frustration.

"You and I have always agreed on that," Pam said thoughtfully.

It was clear she had not chosen this course of action, or inaction. She'd arrived here a few weeks ago and was only beginning to get an understanding of the task ahead of her.

"You have to do something," John said. "If DC is any indicator, the cities are dividing into factions and they are killing each other and anyone who gets in their way. You've got to step in, you've got to stop the violence."

"Yes, and I need your help," Pam said, as if she had predicted that this would be his plea.

"My help?" John asked.

"I want you to be my vice-president. I want you to help me begin the process of rebuilding—no, it's more than that—of healing what's left of our nation," Pam said to John.

"I'm … I'm not qualified," he said.

"You are qualified in the ways it matters," she said. "I remember the first day I met you, I was struck by your humility. That's a rare quality anywhere, but especially in politics. You have no idea how refreshing it was to see a young politician there, not because he could get something out of the office, but because he believed he could give something to it."

"That was a lifetime ago," John said. "Besides, have you forgotten—you and I rarely agreed on anything."

"We agreed when it counted," she said. "We agreed that government was there to serve the people. That elected officials were called to put themselves last, not first. And we agreed that our nation was founded as a democracy and should remain as such. These were the core issues that united us and they are what matters most, especially now. Yes, we disagreed on most other issues, but isn't there value in that? Isn't there value in civil disagreement, in true intellectual debates?"

"I believe so," John said hesitantly.

"So do I," Pam said. "I don't want someone by my side who tells me I'm right. That's one of the things I loved most about my husband." Her voice conveyed the pain of her loss. "He told me when I was wrong and when I was right. And I did the same with him. We were honest with one another and we had an amazing marriage because of it.

I think if you and I can do the same when it comes to rebuilding our nation, we can do really good things."

"It will take a massive amount of work," John said.

"Could there be a better way to spend a life?" Pam asked, repeating his words from earlier.

His eyes left hers.

"What is it?" she asked.

He hesitated. "Juliette is alive."

"You found her!" Pam exclaimed.

"Who is Juliette to you?" Jael asked, with an edge of protectiveness.

"His daughter," I said.

"Say what?" Ash said.

John nodded. "She's my daughter. She helped East and Haz escape DC, and now she's gone to North Carolina with East's family," John said to Pam.

Jael and Ash were both leaning back in their chairs, and Pam was leaning forward.

"John, that's amazing! What about Camille and Johnny?" Pam asked with cautious hope.

"I don't know," he said, "but Juliette will."

I cringed on the inside, sure that they were dead. Juliette never would've left the city if her mom and brother were there, and if they were somewhere else she wouldn't have stayed with us. She would have gone to search for them.

"Yes, Juliette will know," Pam said. "This is amazing. After all this time, she survived. Why on earth are you here? Why haven't you gone to her?"

A pang of guilt stabbed my chest.

John said, "It wasn't until the end of our time in DC that we figured out their friend and my daughter were the same person. And we needed to come here and share the knowledge we had of DC with you. From here, we will go there."

"In other words, Haz and East wouldn't take you to her until after you all came here?" Ash said, in an accusing tone that he tried to disguise as funny.

"We weren't trying to be mean," I said.

"It doesn't matter if you were trying, you succeeded," Jael scolded. "You don't keep a man from his daughter, and you especially don't keep that precious girl from her father."

"You would've set the mission aside and taken him to her?" Haz asked, already knowing the truth.

Jael and Ash said nothing. It was Pam who next spoke.

"John, why did you tell me Juliette was alive in a way that made it seem that her existence somehow disqualified you from being vice-president?"

"I need to go to her," he said.

"Of course you do!" Pam said emphatically. "And it needs to be soon. But then you should bring her back here."

"Here?"

"Or to DC. We will be leaving tomorrow to secure it. Once it's safe, you two can live there and be part of the rebuilding," she said.

"You want me to bring her back here?" John asked.

"You're going to DC tomorrow?" Haz asked. His love for that town was easily felt.

"Yes, and yes," Pam replied. "Bring her here. It will be safe, as safe as anywhere, perhaps more so because we should be able to get power restored to most of the city within the year. We've been waiting for the navy to secure their ships, and they will be in place tonight. We'll go tomorrow. Hopefully, we won't need the ships."

"It's best to be prepared," Jael said.

Pam nodded. "That's what the admiral kept advising me."

"Is the navy in a position of strength?" I asked, remembering the rusting tank at Quantico that sat in the middle of a deserted field.

"The ships that were at sea last Thanksgiving were all far enough away from the EMPs that they're not damaged," Pam said. "Those that were at port are mostly dead in the water, though the manual weapons obviously remain and could be somewhat useful if an attacker came close enough. Thankfully, and tragically, we are in no worse of a state than any other previously developed nation, so we are not particularly concerned about outside invaders."

"Are you going to bomb DC?" I said, keeping my voice calm though I felt a sense of dread.

"As a last resort," Pam said. "And even then, it's extremely unlikely. Our hope is to be able to convince the leaders to lay down their arms. If that doesn't work, we'll use force, but not from the sky. The risk of hitting innocents is too great."

Pam leaned forward, her hands flat on the polished table. "Will you come with us, John, to talk sense into the false leaders in DC? If you do, I will allow Air Force Two to take you and anyone else who wants to go, to North Carolina so you can bring Juliette here. Then there will not actually be a delay in your getting to her. The helicopter will get you there in hours instead of days or weeks."

"Will you only give me a helicopter if I agree to be vice-president?" John asked cautiously.

Pam met his eyes. "It would no longer be Air Force Two if you were not the vice-president, but I would still allow you to use a helicopter. I could never deny any assistance I could give to Juliette."

John hesitated and looked up at the screens showing deserted cities that nature was taking back, contrasting with the scenes of mass death.

He lowered his gaze and closed his eyes. He opened them a moment later. "I would be honored to be the vice-president of the United States of America."

Eighteen
EAST

"This place is strange," I said to Jael as we each lay on our bunk.

"Strange, how?" she said. The bed beneath mine shook as she rolled to her side.

"I'm lying on a soft bed with clean sheets, I took a hot shower, I had rice and canned tomatoes with beef for dinner. It was seasoned with salt and pepper. There was hot sauce on the table for anyone who wanted it. This place is strange."

She laughed. "You mean it reminds you of your life before the attack?"

"Yeah," I said. "And it makes me uneasy."

There was no campfire between us, no dirt at our feet. The door was made of steel and locked from the inside. We were safe and that was unsettling.

"It took me a minute to get used to it, when I first came here. You'll adjust," she said.

"I'm not sure I want to."

"You like living in the woods, sleeping on dirt?" Jael asked.

My eyes were adjusting to the darkness. Do I like those things? "I like the freedom the woods offer," I answered. "I feel trapped here in this steel cave."

"You can leave at any time," she said.

"I didn't say I *was* trapped, I said I *felt* trapped."

"Relax, we leave in the morning, and even *you* can survive one night of civilization," Jael said as I heard her shift onto her back.

I stared at the ceiling, the faint red light of the smoke detector illuminating the square tiles around it. The smell of bleach emanated from the white pillowcase and sheets that surrounded me. There were many smells I missed from my previous life; bleach wasn't one of them.

"Have you seen him?" I asked into the darkness.

"Who?"

"Derrick. Have you seen him or spoken with him?" I wasn't sure what I wanted the answer to be or if there was a point in knowing.

"Yes," she said, her teeth sounding close together. "When we first got here, he greeted us like he was king of the castle."

My breath came faster as the anger increased.

"He told the others who Pam was. She was one of the many they were waiting for."

"Did she know she was in line for the presidency?" I asked.

"Yes, but she was like number thirty or forty on the list, so it's not like she ever thought she would actually be president. But once he told them, they immediately took a DNA sample, her identity was confirmed, and she was sworn in. As soon as the ceremony was over, she ordered him locked up," Jael said with minimal satisfaction. "I haven't seen him since. Haven't wanted to."

"I'm still surprised Pam didn't have him shot," I said.

"Ash suggested that in his typical not subtle way, and she said enough people had already died."

I nodded my head against my pillow, though Jael would not know that.

"Did he say why he did it?" I asked.

I heard the sheets rustle as she moved. "As he was being hauled off, he was shouting, saying stuff about how we should thank him because now we have a chance, now we will work together, now we can get back to our roots— lies like that."

"Do you think he believed them?"

Jael hesitated. "Yes," she said, "I think extremists almost always believe the lies they spread."

"What did Pam say?"

"Nothing. She looked sick, like she was trying not to vomit, and went to her quarters. When she came back about an hour later, her eyes were red, but she was all business and all focus. Since then, she's never stopped working except to sleep a few hours each night. I'm glad John said yes to being the V.P. She needs the help and she needs someone she feels she can trust."

"Do you think that's what went wrong? People stopped trusting each other?"

She was silent. I pulled the covers up. The room was colder than I was used to sleeping in during the summer.

"Yes," Jael finally said in the quiet of the steel cage we slept in. "I think people stopped trusting each other, but before that they stopped listening to each other and stopped respecting each other. I also think the majority of people really want to be led. If their leaders are good, they are led to good, but if they are not, then they are not. If our leaders lack virtue and are too selfish or spineless to defend the weak, how can we expect those they lead to be any different."

"What if it wasn't the leaders' fault?" I asked. "What if the people were simply electing people like themselves?"

I heard a clicking of the metal beneath my mattress and I envisioned her picking at the thick wires that supported it.

"Before the EMPs I felt the world was out to get me," she confessed.

"I felt the same," I said, feeling tired at the thought of those memories.

"Yeah, and you and me, we couldn't have been more different. You, a rich white kid from the South, going to college. Me, a poor black kid from the North, working my butt off in the army. But we felt the same and most everybody I talked to did. People felt like the world was a bad place filled with bad people that were out to get them. But the thing was, I liked the people I was around. I loved my husband and the people we worked with. I loved Momma and the people on her street. I never met those people who were out to get me, but I believed they were there. Sure, there were jerks every once in a while, but mostly, people were nice."

"It was the same for me," I said, wondering now where the fear came from. Yes, Mick was evil, but my fear wasn't about more people like him. By the time I was in college I could easily handle any sort of physical attack. My fear went deeper. Where did it come from?

"It was the same for just about everyone," she said. "People saw the world and our country as bad. We stopped being a people of hope and turned into a people of fear. And that fear produced this."

The air pushed through the vents, creating the sound of electric wind.

I rolled onto my side, the mattress soft beneath my hip. "My grandfather always told me some fear was good. It kept you safe. The rest was from the devil. It kept you controlled."

"I like that. How are you and Jonah related to someone that wise?" she teased.

I laughed. "We always wondered the same thing."

"Humor," she said. "We lost that too. Hope and humor were replaced by anger and fear. And people consumed with anger and fear aren't thinking the same as people who can laugh at themselves and have hope for the future."

"No, they aren't," I said, remembering the few times I watched the news before the attacks. According to the broadcasters, everything in the world was wrong. But that wasn't truth, that was fear, a fear that had taken control of enough people so that Derrick and others like him were able to destroy the country. The country that more than any other country embodied hope. We, her citizens, let fear win and hope die.

***

It was morning now, though I had no way of knowing it other than the clock on the wall and the sounds of soldiers in the hallway. Sunlight, like EMPs, could not penetrate this mountain fortress. As I sat up and dressed, I wondered how the people stationed here had remained sane for the past nine months—living in a glorified cave.

There was a knock on the door.

Haz was there, clean shaven, with fresh clothes on. His dimples would've made Josh jealous.

"Good morning, East," he said. "I'm on my way to breakfast and figured I'd see if you and Jael were heading that way."

"Jael's not here, but I'll go with you," I said.

"Great, it's a date," he said.

I made a face before I could stop myself.

Haz laughed. "Gus would give you such a hard time right now. A nice young man asking you to breakfast and your expression is like a skunk just sprayed you."

I closed the door and giggled in spite of myself. "He *would* give me a hard time," I said. "I didn't mean to make that face. I'm grateful we're friends."

"Is that all I am?" he asked.

The rough stone of the hallway kept me from escaping; there was nowhere to go as I walked beside him to the dining hall.

"What else should you be?" I asked, trying to keep my tone light, though I could tell he wasn't joking.

"Friend is all right, but I hope someday it might be more than that." He sounded sincere.

His hope was unrealistic. Jael, as much as she liked to tease me about Haz having feelings for me, reminded me often that Haz would never be okay with the sort of "innocent relationship" I required. And since I would not compromise my standards, she told me clearly that Haz and I would never work, no matter how adorable our children might be.

We stopped outside of the dining hall. "Haz, I respect you and I enjoy being around you, but I'm not the right woman for you."

"What if I disagree," Haz said, his voice strong but nervous.

Vulnerability, weakness of any kind was not something I was used to hearing from him. Sensing weakness in others often brought out the worst in me; it was as if it activated some sort of ancient kill or be killed instinct. But hearing it in Haz's voice did the opposite. It made me want to step closer, to take care of him and protect him from anyone who might hurt him, including me.

"You disagree because you don't know what I expect out of a relationship," I said, silently pleading with him that he would allow us to be friends and nothing more.

He stood straighter, his shoulders broadening, arms folded across his chest. "East, you live your life in a way that makes your expectations perfectly clear. You don't have to speak them. They are known to all those who care to pay attention, and I very much care to pay attention."

I hesitated. I wanted to believe him, but I didn't.

"You're a guy," I said, crossing my arms and standing as tall as I could. "Your expectations are also perfectly clear."

He stepped toward me, his folded arms almost touching mine, the energy surrounding him becoming angry and hurt. "You're right. If you believe that, you aren't the right woman for me."

He turned and pushed open the silver door to the dining hall.

I watched the door swing closed behind him, the sound of clanking silverware traveling from the dining hall to where I stood.

"You doing okay?" a voice asked.

I blinked as if waking from a dream, or maybe nightmare would be more accurate.

"Yeah, Luke, I'm fine," I answered, the smell of food reminding me I was hungry.

"Are you going to breakfast?" he asked.

"Yes," I said, and started toward the door.

He entered beside me. I paid no attention to him as I searched the room for Haz. He was sitting in the center, surrounded on all sides. I took the rations I was given and filled up a glass with ice and fake orange juice.

Jael came beside me. "I'm over here," she said.

I followed her to the table she shared with Ash and as I set my tray down, Haz lifted his head. He didn't see me; he wasn't looking for me.

Luke was at my side. "Mind if I sit here?" he asked.

I didn't respond.

Jael did. "It's a free country, Luke, but I'm telling you you're taking your life into your own hands." She was teasing.

"Why did you say that?" I asked her, my serious tone a contrast to her joking one.

"It was a joke," she said slowly, as if trying to make sure I understood the words.

"Yeah, I know, but why do you joke like that? Why do you make it seem like Haz and I are together and at the same time remind me that we could never be together?" My eyes searched hers.

"Why couldn't you be together?" Ash asked, his mouth full of grits.

"Come on, you know her and you know him," Jael said.

"Yeah." He swallowed. "What's the problem?"

"That's just it, Jael," I said. "I don't think you see him, not really."

A woman who was sitting by Haz stood up.

"I'll be back in a minute," I said abruptly, leaving them and going to Haz.

I slipped into the seat beside him and leaned in toward him, not waiting for him to acknowledge me or ask why I was there sitting so close. "You're right," I said. "You aren't like other guys. It wasn't fair for me to treat you that way."

He put his fork down. "I used to be," he said. "I used to be no better than any of them. I think that's why you comparing me to them made me so angry."

I sat back, putting distance between us, the thought of him with other women making me feel sick, though I had no right or reason to care.

Haz turned to me. "I changed a long time ago, but you aren't wrong to say you deserve more."

"I never said that," I whispered.

"You should," he said, anger replaced by sadness as he leaned back in his chair.

"What changed you?" I asked.

Haz held his hands together in his lap, his arms loose as he lifted his head toward the ceiling. The LED lights were blindingly bright.

"Jazmyne," he said. "She changed everything."

"Jazmyne was a child," I said, praying he had never had romantic feelings for a fourteen-year-old girl.

He sat forward, his hands on his legs, his eyes on mine. "Yes," he said. "And before her, I saw women differently.

213

They weren't objects to me, like they were for a lot of guys, but they weren't much more than that."

I fought the repulsion I felt.

His eyes turned from mine. "When I was trying to save her, I entered the world she was being held in and I saw human girls,"—his voice choked—"girls like Juliette, being treated as …." His eyes welled with tears and his words stopped. He sniffed and held his arms tight around himself, as if holding in the tears. He shook his head, trying to shake away the pain. "I've never even seen animals treated like that." He hit his foot against the floor and rubbed his hands together, loosening his shoulders.

"You don't have to say anything else," I said.

"It needs to be said." He sniffed, making his voice sound as normal as possible. "At first it was easy for me to look at those men who were abusing and raping those girls, as evil and completely different from me and my friends. And then, for some reason, I had the understanding that even though I never did anything as horrible as they did, I wasn't that much better. Not really."

His eyes refocused on mine. "East, I'm not that guy anymore, but I don't blame you for a second if who I was is too much for you."

"Thank you for telling me that," I said, unsure of what else to say.

"Is this it? Is this where you and I end?" he asked.

"I don't want that," I said, my voice soft and scared. This was my true voice, the one few people ever heard. "But I'm not capable of anything more than friendship right now. Maybe someday, a very long time from now, I might be ready for something more, but I don't expect you to be here then. Not because you're flawed, but because you're human and you're ready for a relationship."

My hand moved to touch the side of his face, but I stopped it in midair. "I'm not. Maybe if what happened when I was a kid hadn't happened, maybe then I might be, but as it is, men—even good men—scare me." I stopped, my voice faltering.

He turned toward me. "I've seen that evil," he said, cautiously taking my hand in his. "And if I'm being honest, it destroyed a part of me." He lowered his gaze.

The sound of metal clanking against hard plastic all around us was drowned out by the sound of voices and my racing heart.

Haz said, "I guess what I'm saying is I also need to heal, and maybe, if it's all right, we can be friends and help one another. That's honestly all I want."

"I don't discuss what I've been through with people," I said.

"Me neither," he said, looking down at our hands. "But maybe sometimes we should."

I felt his hand in mine. This was the most intimate I'd ever willingly been with a man.

"That won't be easy for me."

He held my hand tighter. "It won't be easy for me either, but I'm willing to try."

I hesitated, but only slightly. It was time for me to move beyond my past. Time for me to truly be as strong and healthy as the world thought I was.

"Me too," I whispered.

Nineteen
BRIA

I raised my head. The mat Jonah had slept on was empty. I swung my legs from the bed, careful not to wake Gus or Thomas. One of the puppies rolled over and another yawned as they watched me tiptoe out the door. HoneyBee lifted only her eyelids as I slipped outside.

The orange fire glowed bright in the dark grays of the predawn world. I went to the fire pit. Jasper came to me, putting his head on my lap as I sat beside Jonah.

"You're up early," I said to my husband while rubbing the dog's head.

Jonah stretched and kissed me. "I woke up, so I figured I'd get up and get the fire going. Do you want some tea?"

"Tea would be great," I said.

He stood and used a metal hook to retrieve a tea kettle from its stand above the flames. He set it on the stone and used a thick rag to hold the kettle and pour its water into a mug. He sprinkled some dried peppermint leaves into the water and handed me the mug. Its heat warmed my hands. Before he sat, he put the kettle back above the flames. I lifted the mug to my face and inhaled the sweet smell of peppermint.

"It smells wonderful," I said, grateful for the conveniences of town.

He put an arm around my shoulders, and I nuzzled against him.

"You aren't usually awake this early," I said, between sips of tea. The hot peppermint was waking up my mind and body.

He didn't say anything.

"Are you anxious to get going?" I asked.

"Yes," he said.

The town was silent, and from the silence I could hear there was more bothering him.

"What's wrong?" I asked.

He took the mug from me and took a sip of the tea before handing it back to me.

"Something doesn't feel right."

"With you and me?" I asked, worried.

"No. With this whole thing. Now that we're here and a little closer to finding East, I don't feel how I thought I would feel."

"How's that?"

"I've been thinking about finding her since we left her here, and we're close, maybe a day away, maybe less, if Raven Rock is as close as they say. And there is a sense of excitement and happiness, but there's also dread and fear."

"A lot of unknowns separate us from East, even if the distance isn't far," I said, trying to convince us both that it was normal to worry.

"I keep telling myself that, but the fear only grows."

I held the tea, thankful for something to focus on. The fire crackled in front of us; I watched the orange and yellow flames dance against the blackened stone.

"I have the same feeling," I said, finally admitting what I should have told him days ago. "I keep telling myself I'm being ridiculous, but I'm terrified my dad won't live long enough for me to see him again."

Jonah twisted his body to face me. "Why didn't you tell me?"

I shrugged. "Talking about it makes it seem more real and I don't want it to be real."

"Was he that much worse?" Jonah asked with concern.

"He was so thin and pale," I said. "And the way he said goodbye to me, it was the same way my mom said goodbye to me in her journal." I stared at the dirt that surrounded the sneakers I wore, an old pair of my mom's. She had good taste; I would've picked the same ones.

"I was so focused on finding East ..." Jonah said, his expression distraught.

"In some strange way, my dad, being like he was, made it easier for me to leave," I said, my voice catching.

"I didn't want to watch him melt away into nothingness, I didn't want to watch him suffer."

Jonah knelt in front of me, his fingers touching my legs. "I'm sorry," he said.

I blinked until the tears stopped. "As badly as I didn't want to watch him die, he didn't want me there watching. He wanted me to leave."

"He loves you," Jonah said.

"I was being selfish," I said.

"Selfish?" Jonah repeated, his hands on my thighs, his head even with mine.

"I didn't want to watch him die, so I left."

"Nobody wants to watch someone they love suffer and die," he said.

"Yes, but others are strong enough to do it, even though they don't want to. I'm not. That's the difference."

"Bria, you didn't leave to run from your father's death, so stop trying to tell yourself you did. You left to search with me and to be with me. If we were home, you would be beside your dad, during his good days and bad days. Because that is who you are."

"You have such a high opinion of me," I said, trying and failing to smile.

The back of his finger touched my face. "I see you for who you are," he said.

Saying goodbye was never easy, though it was becoming routine.

Leaving the safety of the town and the love of the people there was always difficult, but today was worse because we were leaving a sobbing Sebastian. It was the right decision, but at this moment it felt horrible.

His little tears were so raw, his loss so extreme. In his mind, and in truth, Eli had saved him, rescuing him from the harvesters, and keeping him safe and comforted during our trek here. We didn't know what happened to his parents, but it was likely that Eli had been the first person to show him kindness since he was separated, in one way or another, from them. Now the boy was being asked to separate from Eli.

We thought at first that Beau's staying might help Sebastian, but Sebastian hadn't connected with Beau; his presence did nothing to help. Marjorie and Becca were doing the most, each beside him, trying to comfort him. Marjorie's children hugged him and offered him the few trinkets they had, to ease his pain. Other children from town were also attempting to distract and entertain him, but he would not be distracted, he would not be entertained.

Eli knelt on one knee in front of Sebastian, his body still towering above the young boy. "Please try to understand. We have no idea what will happen to us once we leave this town. It truly is not safe for you to come with us. Becca and Marjorie, Beau, and all the others will take wonderful care of you and you will have other children here to play with."

"No, don't leave me," Sebastian said between sobs, the tears and snot mixing as they ran down his face and neck.

Eli sat beside Sebastian and held him close. Gazing up to the heavens, Eli spoke to Sebastian. "Let's make a deal. You stay here and have lots of fun, and when I am somewhere safe that I'm going to stay, I will come get you. By then, you won't want to leave all the fun here. But I promise I'll come for you, and if you still want to come with me, I'll take you with me."

"You pinky promise?" Sebastian asked.

Eli held up his pinky, and Sebastian did the same.

"Pinky promise," Eli said.

Sebastian clasped Eli's pinky and wrapped his arms around Eli. Eli stood while lifting the boy. Sebastian was crying as Eli handed him to Becca, but he allowed Becca to hold him without fighting her.

"Have fun while I'm away and tell me all about it when I get back," Eli called as we quickly started forward.

We had been trying to leave for at least an hour. The poor child. I wondered how he had any tears left.

We were down the hill and crossing the road when I turned to face the direction of the town. I could see no one, but, just in case, I lifted my arm and waved.

"Waving to Sebastian?" Jonah asked, amused.

"I love that you get me," I said, bumping my hip against his.

He leaned forward and kissed me as we walked farther into the open field.

"Becca will take good care of him," Eli said, partially asking our opinions and partially reassuring himself.

"She will take great care of him," I said. "He will be good for her too. She lost her daughter to the sickness that killed Sara's mom and Jael's husband."

Eli said, "I heard whispers of that when I asked Becca to be the one to care for Sebastian."

"Everyone in town will help care for him. He will be loved and safe," Jonah said. "Besides, you couldn't raise him. That's not your station in life."

We entered the woods and instantly felt the air cool. My nerves calmed; I felt safer in the trees.

"It wasn't," Eli said pensively, "but I wonder."

"What do you mean?" Jonah asked with concern. "You aren't thinking of leaving the priesthood."

"No, no," Eli said, as if that thought was ludicrous. "But I wonder if aspects of that have changed. Religious men and women used to run orphanages and still do, in different countries. It was never something that even crossed my mind before, but I wonder now."

"You want to raise kids?" Jonah asked with confused surprise.

"I want to care for those who need caring for," Eli said, to clarify. "Before all of this, I focused on the spiritual needs of those in my congregation, primarily because their physical needs were more than met, but now … there must be others like Sebastian."

"Children without parents?" I asked.

Eli nodded. "Every child deserves what he now has."

"It isn't just about the child," Felicia said, coming from behind us. "There are lots of parents like Becca who have lost children and lots of others who would gladly open their hearts to more."

"Yes, you're right," Eli said, nodding vigorously. "Maybe my role is to help unite children with parents who will love them and raise them as their own."

"That would be a beautiful way to spend a life," Felicia said with deep emotion as she gazed at her daughter.

"Yes," Eli said pensively, "that would be a beautiful way to spend a life."

Jonah slowed his pace and I slowed mine to match; we lagged behind the others now.

"What is it?" I asked in a soft tone.

"Just as I'm trying to bring one sibling home, another one is talking about leaving," he said, sounding defeated.

"Eli."

Jonah nodded.

"He didn't say anything about not being at home."

"He wants to unite kids and parents. He wants to make families. It's awesome, but it can't happen in the middle of the woods, with only our family around," Jonah said sadly.

"I hadn't thought of that," I said.

We walked on in silence, catching up to the group. The conversation between Eli and Felicia wafted over me. She was right. Creating families was an incredible way to spend a life. As Eli became more and more excited, I realized that Jonah was also right. Eli might return home with us, but he would not stay. My heart broke as we trekked through the late summer forest.

I loved Eli, I loved his presence, I loved the peace that surrounded him, and I loved myself when I was near him.

Jonah reached for my hand; I took his. We continued forward together.

Twenty
EAST

My head spun as the elevator carried us to the top of the bunker. I leaned against the back wall, trying to keep the dizziness from overwhelming me. I closed my eyes, reminding myself the feeling would pass once the doors opened—though I was lying to myself. Much of what I was feeling had nothing to do with the elevator and everything to do with my conversation with Haz. I had been more honest than I'd ever been with anyone in my life and that terrified me.

The doors opened and I stepped out of the elevator, following Jael and Ash. The spinning stopped, but the total preoccupation with Haz did not.

Even from deep inside the cave I could tell the outside doors were open. The air smelled different, fresher in a more natural way. Once we turned the corner, the space flooded with sunlight and my mind settled. I was no longer preoccupied with Haz. Interested, yes, but the unease left. I stood taller when we reached the outside, my eyes squinting. I slipped on the sunglasses I'd been given.

The rifle slung across my back, along with the four heavily armed helicopters, banished any remaining worry I felt. However, it felt unnatural not to be carrying a pack.

Jael assured me it was fine; the helicopters carried enough supplies for each of us. I slipped my hand into the pocket of my tan military cargo pants, my fingers brushing the smooth plastic of the lighter. With fire and a weapon, I could survive even without their supplies. This awareness was the only way I'd agreed not to carry my own pack of supplies.

Haz stood beside a helicopter. We went toward him.

"Load up," Jael commanded as she climbed in beside the pilot. The word VENOM was stenciled onto her door.

I followed Ash into the helicopter; Haz and seven others settled in.

"It's too bad Luke couldn't join us," Ash said in a mocking tone.

Neither Haz nor I responded. As the door closed and the blades began to spin, I turned my attention to the window.

Jael signaled for us all to put on headsets. "The navy ships are in place," she said through the headphones.

"The sight of them should end any resistance," Ash said, sounding cocky even through the garbled sound of the headsets.

"Maybe, maybe not," Jael said. "If the resistance on the ground believes they are fighting to protect the US, they'll keep fighting. Our job, or more specifically, the V.P.'s job, is to convince them to lay down their arms."

Marine Two was flying beside us. John was there, along with the military officers who were now functioning as the Secret Service. As we neared DC they would slow, hovering high above until any immediate threats were removed, and we were on the ground.

I closed my eyes, my head resting against the seat.

If this mission was successful and John was able to stop the fighting in DC, then Pam, Madam President, had agreed to allow John to use Marine Two to travel to North Carolina and get Juliette. We would be allowed to travel with him. I opened my eyes and watched the world below fly by. If we were successful, we would be on our way to my parents and Quinn in just a few days. I focused on the blurring trees and rolling mountains, not allowing myself to focus on the hope of seeing my family so soon. The world flew by too quickly. I closed my eyes and ran through scenario after scenario of hand-to-hand combat, mentally practicing the movements my body would make to counter a gun being pointed at my head or a knife against my throat. These thoughts would keep me alive; thoughts of my family would not.

Twenty-One
BRIA

We were in the middle of farmland when I heard the sound. The sound that I once loved and now feared. The sound of helicopters overhead. More than one. My heart raced as we sprinted as fast as we could for the cover of the trees. I dove into the woods, Jonah beside me, the others beside him.

"There's no way they didn't see us," he called over the sound of the machines.

He was right. Two of the helicopters continued on while two hovered above us. I desperately searched for an escape. The trees we were in were only a strip, a slim barrier of wilderness between two giant fields. We could run, but the helicopters could track us, the soldiers shooting us from the sky.

"Be ready to fight," Blaise said.

Everyone readied their guns as the helicopters landed. The lump in my throat was so large it was nearly impossible to breathe. My heartbeat pulsed in my ears, drowning out the sound of whirring blades.

The door to the helicopter closest to us opened.

A gun fired.

Terror gripped me. We were completely outnumbered; we would not win this fight.

"Don't fire!" Jonah shouted, his hand pushing the barrel of Richard's gun toward the ground.

Richard fired?

No one inside the helicopters moved. It must've been him.

A pack was thrown from the helicopter. Richard didn't fire and neither did the rest of us. A person cautiously stepped from the machine, his skin so dark it was difficult to make out his features in the shade of the helicopter.

"Haz?" Blaise shouted, standing as she did so. Josh was trying to pull her down.

Behind the man, a fair-skinned woman stepped from the helicopter.

"East!" Jonah said under this breath as he stood and began running to his sister.

Eli followed. East ran to them. They met in the field, Eli and Jonah lifting East into the air.

"What are you doing here!" she exclaimed in excitement.

Jael and Ash were out of the helicopter and coming toward us.

"We came to find you," Jonah said.

"Find me?" East asked. "You came from home?"

"It was Jonah's idea," Eli said, his arm still around his sister.

"To risk your life?" East asked, her body becoming stiff, the excitement fading.

"I couldn't leave you out here," Jonah said.

"So you selfishly risked the lives of Eli and our friends," she said with anger.

"It was nice, what Jonah did, what we've all done," Eli said, his tone reminding me of Quint's when speaking to his younger children.

"Don't you get it?" East shot back. "Nice doesn't matter. Staying alive—that's what matters."

"Don't you get it?" Blaise said, stepping toward her. "That's what we're doing. We're fully aware of the risks. We couldn't leave the war to you four. The harvesters are only getting closer. We have to stop them."

"Harvesters?" Haz asked.

"That's the made-up name my daughter and her friends use for soldiers," Richard said.

"Soldiers who harvest people," Blaise added.

"There are people harvesting people?" Ash asked in disgust.

"She means they're using them as slaves," Felicia said.

"That's no less disgusting, Mom." Old wounds were evident in Blaise's tone.

"I never said it was," Felicia said. "Only explaining what you were trying to say."

"My words were clear," Blaise said, arms crossed, anger flowing from her to her parents.

"I'm glad you found your parents," Haz said, dimples showing, distracting Blaise.

"I've missed those dimples," Blaise said, touching his face.

Josh shook his head and lovingly pulled his wife toward him.

"Where's Sara?" East asked.

"Sara's fine," Jonah assured her. "She didn't come because Sage is pregnant."

"Pregnant?" Jael said.

"It's a long story," Blaise said.

"The details are long, the synopsis is short," Josh said. "She met a boy, he was with us for a few weeks. She got pregnant, he was a coward and abandoned her when we led a slave revolt. We all hated him for leaving her, until we discovered he murdered his whole family in cold blood. Now we're okay with it and we're hoping the baby doesn't take after him."

"I've missed you, Josh," Ash said, pulling Josh into a hug.

"I've missed you too, man," Josh said, lifting Ash into the air.

"I'm sorry Sage experienced that," East said with sadness.

"We are too," Blaise said.

"The baby will be a blessing," I said softly.

East smiled. "Yes, the baby will be a blessing."

"Where'd you get the helicopters?" Josh asked, reminding me that there was more to this moment than a joyous reunion.

"It's a long story," Jael said.

"The synopsis is short," Ash said, winking. "Turns out the government in DC is a fake. These are the real soldiers and they have plenty of weapons and helicopters and tanks and navy ships. We are on our way to DC to take back the city. Want to come?" His eyes glowed with delight—like a child about to play tag, not a soldier about to attack Washington, DC.

Richard was the first to step forward. "Count me in," he said.

Blaise, Josh, and Felicia followed.

"I won't fight," Eli said.

"Of course you won't, my dear priest brother," East said, slipping her arm through his.

"Your brother's a priest?" Haz said, sounding embarrassed and intimidated.

Eli wrapped his arm around East, and she did the same with him. Haz went with them went to the helicopter. Only Jonah and I were left.

"What do you think?" Jonah asked.

"We came here to bring East home," I said. "We haven't accomplished that yet."

He took my hand in his and we began walking slowly to the helicopter. "No, we haven't," he said. His hand was tight around mine, his thumb rubbing the outside of my hand in the way he did when he was feeling anxious.

"We have the backing of the actual military," I said, trying to calm him.

"It's not that. There's something else," he said. "The pit in my stomach keeps growing."

"It's a lot to take in," I said, trying to convince both of us there was nothing to fear.

The door closed behind us. We sat on the floor, in front of Haz and East. It didn't matter that the floor of the helicopter was hard metal; it was far better than walking all the way to DC.

As we flew, Haz and, sometimes, East told us of their time in DC, and of how the man in the other helicopter was both Juliette's dad and the vice-president of the United States. It made sense that Juliette would be the daughter of the vice-president. Though she didn't know it, she exuded aristocracy, even with a rifle strapped to her back.

"We promised John," East yelled above the wind, "that we would leave DC soon, a week, tops."

"He was only okay with that," Haz shouted, "because Pam, who is now the president, promised him we could take a helicopter to Juliette."

"I would've been on my way home in a week," East said, arms crossed in anger as she glared at Jonah.

Eli kicked her from his seat across from us.

"He did a good thing," Eli said. "The proper response is 'Thank you.' "

Haz leaned his head toward East, his cheek brushing her white-blonde hair, and said, "I like him."

She sat up straighter and smiled. "I do too."

I sat back, leaning against the metal wall of the helicopter. Even if we stayed in DC for a month, we would be home long before the snow. The corners of my lips lifted involuntarily.

"What're you thinking about?" Jonah asked.

"I won't have to eat a rotten apple," I yelled over the roar of the blades.

"JP?" East asked, one eyebrow raised.

I nodded. "He wasn't happy we left."

"What about Mom and Dad?" she asked.

"No one was happy about us leaving, but none of them tried to stop us. They want you home," I yelled.

She leaned back against the seat, her face titled up, her eyes closed. For the briefest of moments I sensed she was happy we were with her and relieved she would be going home soon.

Twenty-Two
EAST

From the air, the forces inhabiting DC looked as small as they actually were. The so-called rebels and government sides were facing the navy ships in the Potomac. It was like watching insects try to defeat a human. The two opposing forces were not united, but they were working together to attack their shared enemy, truth. Did they realize their time of control was over? That the rightful stewards of this place had returned to claim their land and their people?

Haz handed me a pair of binoculars. I took them and scanned the area beneath us for what he wanted me to see.

Men and women in government uniforms were fighting on both the rebel and fake government sides.

"The government forces splintered?" I yelled, over the racket of the blades.

He nodded.

I lifted the binoculars to my eyes and continued to scan the area. I couldn't see anyone close enough to recognize their face. I scanned for slave clothes. There were lots, all on the side of the rebel forces. Were any of them the freedom fighters? I focused harder on those in slave clothing. It was difficult to tell. If they were there, I didn't see them.

I handed Haz the binoculars and relaxed my eyes, leaning my head against the metal.

"What did you see?" Jonah asked from his spot at my feet.

"The fake government is falling," I answered.

He said nothing and neither did Bria. Should we be excited? I wasn't sure.

I could understand the wisdom in Raven Rock not attacking sooner and allowing those in DC to destroy themselves, but how many lives had been lost as a result of their delay? I leaned back. They didn't care. That was the truth of it, and that was difficult to accept. Pam hadn't been in Raven Rock long. Perhaps I couldn't assign blame to her, but those who'd been there before her could've acted and didn't.

Haz sat beside me. This was why he chose to work for the system—to be a voice of reason among chaos. He left when the chaos became too great and reason could no longer be heard. When I stayed in the town with him, I made the same choice: to do whatever I could to help decrease the chaos. I wondered now if it mattered.

To stay here fighting meant leaving my family vulnerable, or at least more vulnerable than they'd be with my protection. Bria's legs were folded up, her arms stretched across her knees. On her left hand she wore a ring. I'd seen it once before, when I was a child. I had found it carefully wrapped in my mother's jewelry box. She told me it belonged to her best friend, the woman whose name I shared, and that one day she hoped to give it to her friend's only living child, a little girl not much older than me. When I asked where the little girl was, my mother took the ring back from me and put it away in her closet. She tried to hide her tears but I saw them.

I never found the ring again.

Beside Bria, Jonah wore a ring of twisted metal. He'd made it himself, I had no doubt. I turned and faced the window. When Jonah left to go home with Bria and the others, I'd felt abandoned. It wasn't fair to feel that way, I knew, but it was how I felt. Everyone was paired up; even Sara had Sage. That didn't matter. I wasn't made for that life. Still, it hurt when my brother chose a girlfriend over me.

It was the right choice. She is his wife now; they are a family. He was choosing to protect that family. That is his role, his primary job in life. Why was he here now, risking his life and hers?

He came here for me. It was a poor decision, but I appreciated it. Any remnant of anger I felt toward him faded as the truth of my thoughts sunk in. He wanted me home. My parents wanted me home. I wanted to be home.

Haz's eyes were on me. He would not choose the quiet country life; his home was this city. His allegiance was to her. I swallowed. I would never ask him to change it.

The helicopter carrying John flew lower, but not low enough to be hit by small arms fire. I wondered what John thought of what he was seeing. He had brought his family here and that choice likely killed his wife and son. Yet, when Pam asked him to stay and rebuild the country, he said yes. He agreed to bring his daughter into this place; he believed that much in the possibility of "better." The freedom fighters were the same. We asked them—I practically begged them to come with us, out of DC. They refused. All of these people saw something I didn't.

Our helicopter turned and went to the far part of town, away from the fighting and the soldiers. The other three followed. In minutes all four helicopters were on the ground, and we were climbing from them and running to deserted buildings.

The helicopters lifted off and flew out of the city.

"If we need the helicopters, I'll call them," Jael said. She carried a radio on her back.

"We're not going to need them," Ash said in his cocky voice.

"What's the plan?" Blaise's father asked.

"They watched us land," Jael said. "Some of their troops will head this way. Once that happens, the navy will begin firing on those that remain on the shore. If the shore clears, they will land and move further inland. The goal is to keep them from leaving the city, and then come back and attack in the future."

"We'd rather finish it here," Ash said.

"By killing them all?" Bria asked.

In frustration, I asked her, "Have you always been such a pacifist?"

Bria said nothing, but Eli turned from me as if disappointed. My face flushed with anger.

"This is a just war," I said, my voice rising. "We have every right to fight, and to kill, if that is what's needed to save the innocent and our country."

Eli must already know that or he wouldn't be here. Which meant he and Bria weren't opposed to the war, they just didn't want to be the ones fighting in it.

Jonah was about to say something when Jael stepped in front of him.

"John is going to speak and try to convince as many as possible to surrender," she said.

I said, "But if that doesn't work, we're ending this."

"Their forces have united," Haz said.

Ash laughed. "The enemy of my enemy is my friend."

We spread out. I peered around a corner. In the far distance I could detect movement.

"They must know we're with the actual government," Bria said. "How else would we have those helicopters or troops."

"Or giant navy ships," Haz added in an amused tone. "Seems the freedom fighters were right. Both sides are equally corrupt."

"Who are the freedom fighters?" Eli asked.

"Some kids we met," I answered.

My hand tightened on my gun. These people were not interested in who the rightful rulers of DC were; they were interested only in power.

They would not allow this to end without death.

Twenty-Three
BRIA

Though we were no longer in the air, my mind was still whirling. Less than an hour ago we were journeying to Raven Rock with hopes of maybe finding East. Now she stood beside me in the heart of DC, and we again gathered around a war table—actually, a picnic table hidden behind a building, with maps of DC sprawled across its surface.

"What are we going to do?" I asked, holding Jonah's hand.

"*You* are going to stay here," East commanded, looking at all of us who came to find her.

Josh said, "We came to protect you."

Jael laughed far too loudly.

"Josh, I love you," East said, sounding tired. "I love each of you, but I don't need protecting. I need this war to be over."

Felicia said, "We didn't come here to hide behind a building."

Jael stepped forward and said, "Those who want to fight can fight. Like East said, we need this war to be over. With more who are fighting with us, that will happen sooner. Haz will be your commander."

She left and went toward the larger group of soldiers. Haz was already there, near Ash.

East shook her head in frustration at all of us, or maybe just at life. "You're fools," she mumbled, before following Jael.

"That went well," Josh said sarcastically.

"Did you think she would be happy we were risking our lives to find her?" Blaise said, leaning against the building.

"She's grateful," Eli said, watching his sister. "She's always cared more about others than herself. She's afraid we'll get hurt."

"Please," Josh said, trying to make light of the situation. "What could possibly go wrong. We're only trying to take the city back from rogue rebels that have told everyone they are the rightful government of the United States. There's no danger in that at all."

We all laughed. It was a nervous sort of laughter, but it still felt good to release some of the tension.

After a few minutes Haz returned, East by his side. "Those of you with us, come on. We're going to find some friends of ours."

"What sort of friends?" Jonah asked as we lifted our packs.

"Kids we met when we were in the city before. They might have some knowledge that could help us keep this from turning into a war that's won by the side that can kill the most people," Haz said. He moved forward, away from Jael and the rest of the soldiers.

"Even though we would win that war," East added, "killing half the population of DC is not the goal."

"They won't be far from here," Haz said, mostly to East.

"No," she replied, and smirked. "Knowing them, they will be way too close."

We followed, weaving through buildings and avoiding soldiers or rebels or whatever they were called, just as we had last time we were here. I thought for the briefest of moments of Trent and my mind moved on. His control over me was gone; the pain of the past remained solidly in the past.

Instead, memories of my childhood occupied my mind. This was my home—not a happy one, but a home nonetheless. The buildings were different and yet the same. When we first came through DC the earth was black and barren. I touched the bark of a cherry tree that I passed and noticed small green leaves. Nature was fighting back. Beneath our feet, grass and weeds had pushed through the cracks and around the edges of the sidewalks.

There was another reason this part of DC did not remind me of Trent; this was not where he had captured me. This was where I had grown up. These were the parks

I'd played in and the streets I'd wandered, feeling alone and unloved. I stopped in front of a sedate brick building. We were close to the White House, where buildings were not allowed to be tall.

"What is it?" Jonah asked.

"This was my dad's apartment," I said, surprised at how emotional my voice sounded as I spoke the words.

Blaise said, "I didn't recognize it."

The windows were broken and chunks of brick were missing, probably from bullets.

"This is where you grew up?" Jonah asked softly.

I nodded, staring up at the building. The front door was splintered from someone forcing it open. Had it been Trent? Had he been the one to force the door to the building open?

"Let's check it out," East said.

It was a kind gesture. She could tell I wanted to go in but lacked the courage to make the decision.

She went first. I followed, Jonah's hand in mind, reminding me of how I held Sara's hand when we had entered her mother's apartment. Would things be as unchanged here as they were there? We climbed along the marble staircase to the second floor, which was my father's apartment. The door was closed. East made eye contact with me. I swallowed and gave a slight nod. She pushed the handle and stood aside, allowing Haz to go first.

After a few moments, Haz said to us, over his shoulder, "Think we're good."

We entered.

Blaise placed her arm around my back, her hand resting on my hip, as I tried to process what I saw. The place had been ransacked. It must have happened soon after the light because whoever was here was looking for something more than food, and once the significance of the light was understood, food was all that mattered.

I stepped forward, Blaise and Jonah releasing me. I went toward my room. They were following me. The room was dark. Instinctively I reached for the light switch. My hand was halfway to it before I let it fall, remembering the switch would do nothing. I crossed the room and opened the drapes. The sunlight reflected off the crystal chandelier, creating flickering rainbows on my walls.

"I always loved that chandelier," I said to Jonah.

He was leaning against the doorframe, watching me. "It's beautiful," he said.

"Yes," I said. "I picked it out when I was nine, when we moved to this apartment. Before that, we lived in a smaller one much further away."

"I'm sure this place wasn't cheap," Jonah said, his eyes not leaving me.

"Twelve million dollars," I said, not hiding the sadness that this place evoked.

Jonah stumbled, catching himself. That was the reason I knew the cost of the apartment. My father wanted everyone to know how much he'd paid for it. He wanted everyone to stumble at the thought of him having that much money. It was important to him that everyone know how much money he had and how quickly he'd made it. I questioned now if anyone from our old life ever wondered what that money had cost Holt Ford and his young daughter. No, I doubted it. My father didn't surround himself with people who would care about such a cost.

My room had not been turned over like the living room, which made it worse. It looked exactly as it had the last time I'd been there. I ran my fingers along the wall and went into the closet. It was almost the same size as the room. The two together could have held most of the apartment Sara shared with her mom and sister—though the love their apartment held would have overwhelmed this place of stoic discontent.

Jonah followed me into the closet. A few drawers sat open. I felt the fine fabrics before closing the drawers. My clothes hung as I'd left them; shoes and purses filled a full wall. I went to the shoes. None of them were of any use now.

"Do you miss it?" Jonah asked, as if apologizing for all he would not be able to give me.

Even if the attacks had not happened, this way of life was one very few had and not one that he would choose even if he could.

"It wasn't a happy life," I said, my fingers gliding across the blouses, some costing thousands, all costing hundreds. My foot kicked something as I turned. I bent down and picked up a crumbled piece of yellow legal paper. I pulled the paper apart. The scribbled handwriting was visible.

"It's from my dad," I said, showing it to Jonah.

Bria,

I don't know what it means if you're reading this. I left to find you. Your mom told me to go home. She meant the home we shared with her. I'm heading there now. All I have is my road bike. If I don't make it, I'm sorry I decided to be your father too late. I love you, I always have.

Please forgive me.
Dad

I smoothed it, tenderly tracing the words my father wrote to me many months ago.

"Why was it crumpled up?" Jonah asked, touching the note in my hands.

"Why is any of the house the way it is?" I asked, and Trent's name entered my mind.

Did he do this? He told me he came here when the light happened. Was he the one who destroyed my father's apartment?

I stared past Jonah. Behind him were the dresses I used to wear, some modest, most not, all costing more than Jonah's car.

"It doesn't matter," I said, refocusing on my husband. "The destruction of this place doesn't matter."

"It was your home," Jonah said.

"No," I said, "it's where I lived. The first *home* I had was the one I shared with you and your family. I was miserable here. All the beautiful clothes and shoes can't hide that."

"I'm sorry," he said, his arms going around me.

I held on to him. "It's in the past." I squeezed him tighter, trying to remind myself that the pain of this place no longer existed. The man and the girl who lived here no longer existed. "Promise me," I said, my face buried in his chest, "that we will grow old together in a home filled with love."

His arms were strong around me, his cheek resting on my head. "I will do everything in my power to make that happen."

As I listened to the steady beat of his heart, I wished just this once he could lie to me. I wished he could tell me it would all be okay, and I wished I could believe it.

Twenty-Four
EAST

Blaise and Bria held hands as we left Bria's dad's apartment.

I wanted to tell Bria it would be okay, that it was her past, and her future with my brother would be better, but I said nothing. Some people would see how rich she was as a gift, and in some lives it was, but not in hers. In hers it attracted guys like Trent.

I was grateful she wore the ring my mother had saved for her, thankful my brother wore one too. They deserved each other: two amazingly good people in a dark world.

"The kids we're looking for," Richard asked. "What do you think they know?"

I bristled at his use of the word "kids" when describing the freedom fighters. I called them that, but I knew them. He didn't, and he shouldn't.

Haz answered, "We're hoping they know who's double crossing who, or who will listen to reason."

"Anything that can help us convince the fake leaders to put down their weapons and allow the rightful government to step back in," I added as we stepped out onto the street.

As we crossed a street we could see lots of activity near the White House. We ducked behind a building. There was a rally of sorts. A voice boomed over a loudspeaker. A voice I recognized.

"We cannot allow these invaders to harm our nation's capital."

Jonah put his arm around Bria as she shivered. The voice belonged to Trent's commander.

"He has no power," I said to Bria. "Don't let his being here mess with your head."

She nodded, but looked like a terrified child.

A rock hit the ground in front of me. I aimed my gun, crouching low, finding the target. The others dove behind the metal garbage container beside us. Only Haz and Richard remained.

Beside me, Haz started to laugh. He lowered his weapon and poked my shoulder, pointing to a second-story window. "Told you they could take care of themselves," Haz said. "Y'all can come out. We found the freedom fighters."

From the window Amber's red hair was visible. Xander and Harley were with her, guns held casually. Haz was right; they could take care of themselves.

The door opened as we neared the building. Haz and I went first into the dark space, the others following. Our eyes adjusted; it wasn't dark but it wasn't well lit either. Most of the windows were covered by blinds or cardboard.

"I told Amber you'd be back," Nevaeh said, excited we were there.

I liked her the best. Less edgy than Amber, far more cautious than Xander and Harley. The only reason she wasn't one of their leaders was because she was so much younger than the others.

"Come on," Xander said. "We can see better upstairs."

"Don't they care who the rest of us are?" Blaise whispered. "We could be bad guys they don't know."

"They've always been too trusting," I grumbled.

Xander chuckled. "That's never how anyone has ever described a bunch of military ex-foster kids."

"Maybe not," I said, "but it's true."

Once we were upstairs, the others came forward.

"They did fine. Everyone's here," Haz said to me, relief in his voice.

"By the grace of God," I said under my breath.

"Probably," Haz said, agreeing with me.

Amber said, "We guessed you might be in those helicopters."

"*We*?" Harley said.

"Whatever," Amber said, rolling her eyes. "I was hoping, okay?" she said, with attitude.

"I'm glad you were hoping, Amber," Haz said sweetly. "Thanks for throwing that rock at us. We were trying to find you."

"Find us? Why?" she said.

Haz crossed through open workspaces to the far side of the building, which faced the White House. He peered cautiously through a slit between the plantation shutters. "We were right," he said. "The government down there isn't the real government."

"We already knew that," the youngest boy, Mason, said.

"How?" I asked.

"They ran out of supplies," Xander said with a smirk.

Mason said, "And half the troops deserted."

"Mason has always exaggerated," Xander said.

"I don't exaggerate, I stink at math," Mason shouted back.

"And he struggles with anger," Harley said, causing Mason to storm off.

"Where did the troops go?" Richard asked, ignoring the squabbling.

"Who are you?" Harley asked, arms crossed.

"Her father," Richard said, with an edge of immature defiance.

"Who's she?" Xander responded.

"She's a friend," I said. "These are her parents and her husband. These two are my brothers and she's my sister-in-law."

Bria and Jonah both looked surprised, as if I was so oblivious that I would miss the fact that they were both wearing rings.

"Thank you for helping us," Felicia said nicely, mimicking Haz's polite tone.

The three leaders exchanged a glance.

"Some left the city, others went into hiding," Xander said, answering Richard's question.

Amber said, "A few joined the rebellion, but not many."

"Do you think those that stayed in the government forces know it's fake?" Haz asked.

"The ones who stayed are the cruelest," Nevaeh said.

"Yeah, they know," Amber said. "They stayed for the power and they're awful."

"We are now rooting for the rebellion," Xander said.

"They aren't much better," Nevaeh said, "just less awful than the others."

"You said the government here is fake?" Harley said.

"How do you know?" Xander said, finishing his thought.

"We found the real thing," Haz said.

"Where?" Nevaeh asked, the others paying closer attention, even Mason, who returned from his brooding spot in a corner.

"Raven Rock," I answered. "Like we hoped."

"Hiding like cowards," Harley said, arms folded.

"Not exactly," Haz said.

"Hiding like cowards would've been better. As it was, they were merely waiting for the forces on the ground to kill each other off," Blaise said, only slightly under her breath.

"Swell," Xander said. "That's a government I can really get behind."

"It's better now," Haz said. "The guy, John, who was with us before, he's the new vice-president. And his friend is the president. John is uptown with troops, preparing to take back the city."

"Then why are you here looking for us?" Mason asked.

"We thought you could tell us who to target, either with words or bullets," Haz said.

The freedom fighters faced one another with thoughtful expressions.

Xander replied, "There's not a lot of reasoning on the government side of things."

"There might be some hope on the rebel side," Amber said.

"The leaders are jerks," Harley said. "But most of the others are there to fight the fake government."

"There are a few on the fake side who've been kind to us," Nevaeh said hesitantly. "I would hate for them to be killed."

"We don't want to kill anyone," Bria, always the pacifist, said.

"We'll do what needs to be done," Haz countered. "Though, hopefully, that means confiscating their weapons and asking them to leave the city."

"Will you come with us?" I asked the freedom fighters.

They exchanged glances.

Amber said, "If we pick a side and that side loses, we'll be targeted."

"Not picking a side has its drawbacks too," Richard cautioned in a slightly threatening way.

The tone in the room changed. The freedom fighters stepped back, if not physically, emotionally.

"That isn't fair," Eli said, stepping toward the fighters. "Their generation didn't create this mess. They shouldn't have to fix it."

"Of course it isn't fair," Richard said. "Life isn't fair. These kids know that better than any of us. Society wrote them off. It didn't care about them."

Eli bristled. "Society cared."

Richard laughed an angry false laugh. "Ask them, ask them how much people cared," he challenged.

Eli paused. One of Eli's best traits was how easily he could control his temper.

"Society should have cared," he said calmly.

"Yes," Felicia said, "it should have."

"It didn't because it didn't have to," Richard said. "If they want it to care now, they need to pick a side and engage, not hide on the outskirts."

"Hiding has kept them alive," Jonah said, stepping toward Richard.

Jonah did not have the same gift of anger control as Eli, nor did he want it.

"Yes, alive," Richard said, "but nothing more. Surviving day to day, which, until now may have been all anyone could ask, but that's changing if they want to be part of it. To get their fair share they need to stop hiding."

The freedom fighters were listening attentively to the back-and-forth.

Amber stepped forward. "He's right. Nobody cared before and nobody cares now."

"Don't be so dramatic, Amber," Nevaeh said. "People cared before, just not as much as we needed them to."

I fought the tears that threatened to come. Her words were not meant to invoke emotion, only to convey the truth; but the truth was devastating.

"Will you help us change that?" Haz asked. "The man you met before, John, is charged with rebuilding the world, or at least our part of it. I've agreed to help him. Will you trust us enough to help us?"

"You've agreed to help him?" I asked, fighting to keep my voice even.

Haz swallowed. "Yes," he said, as if apologizing, though he had nothing to apologize for.

I nodded. What else could I do? What else could I expect? He loved this city; his parents were buried in this city. His telling me he had feelings for me didn't change any of that, and the way I felt about him or my desire to go home certainly didn't. My brothers and Blaise were watching me. They heard the hurt in my voice.

"We need to get moving," I said. "Jael will be expecting us back. Are you in or what?"

The kids looked at each other.

"We're in," Amber said.

***

We split up. Eli, Felicia, Blaise, and Josh stayed with the freedom fighters. The rest came with Haz and me, back to the main team. Those that stayed did so to oversee things from the freedom fighters' hideout. It was a good location, one that would allow them to monitor the fight and enter it if needed, targeting those that the fighters told them to target. With them staying, it also kept the freedom fighters from entering the fight. Though that point had not been spoken of in front of the kids, we understood it was the goal.

From the vantage point of their hideout, Blaise could still use the sniper rifle she'd been given, and Felicia and Eli could ensure that none of the kids crept into the battle.

As we approached from the south, John asked, "Where's the rest of your group?"

"They stayed with the freedom fighters," Haz said.

"You found them." John's voice had lightened.

It was funny to me how much each of us cared for that group of obnoxious kids.

Haz laughed. "Are you kidding? They found us."

"Of course they did," John said, sounding happy for the first time since we'd arrived at Raven Rock. "Were they all there?"

"Yes," I answered. "They've taken over the top floor of that building." I pointed toward their location, careful not to be too specific in case my actions were being watched.

"Why did the others stay?" Jael asked. "I planned on using Blaise as a sniper."

"I'll take her spot," Blaise's dad answered.

"Are you any good?" Ash asked skeptically.

Jonah answered, "He's as good as Blaise, but he shoots to kill."

"Even better," Jael answered.

Bria flinched. I was glad Eli and Sara weren't around to hear that. They would advocate for people to be shot but not killed, which they foolishly believed to be more humane. As if dying from an infection or starving to death as your body tried to heal was somehow better than dying with dignity on the battlefield.

"Did the freedom fighters tell you anything we should know?" John asked, ignoring the conversation between Jael and Richard about where he would be positioned.

Haz said, "The rebels and so-called government forces have splintered and many have deserted."

I said, "The kids don't have much hope for the fake government forces peacefully ending the fight."

"They believed there might be more success with the rebel forces," Jonah added.

"It's going to be tricky to know who's fighting for who," John said thoughtfully.

Ash rejoined our conversation. "If they're shooting at you, shoot back," he said without a hint of fear.

"It's possible it may be that simple," Haz said. "From what we could tell, all the forces are uniting against us."

"Yes," Jael said, turning to us as Richard left. "That's what we're hearing as well."

"Are all of them coming here or are some staying to fight the navy?" Jonah asked.

Jael answered. "From what we've been told, most are heading to us and taking their sweet time. About a hundred stayed on the bank."

"What are they waiting for?" Bria asked, trying to keep her voice from sounding scared.

"Nightfall, I'm sure," Ash answered.

I fought the urge to groan. It was barely past noon.

Twenty-Five
Bria

Dusk was approaching. We'd received intelligence that the troops that were coming to fight us were nearing. They remained out of our sight. However, they were undoubtedly close enough to be seen by the freedom fighters and our friends who'd stayed with them.

John was near us. The communications specialist that traveled with him was finishing setting up the speaker and microphone. The hope we all shared was that our new vice-president, Juliette's father, would be able to win this war with words instead of weapons. I watched the specialist flip switches on: one for the speaker, another for the radio transmitter. If there were any working radios, John's voice would be broadcasted on them.

The microphone buzzed to life. The specialist handed it to the vice-president. He took it from her with caution, as if handling something dangerous and powerful. We'd known him only a few hours; still, it was clear he was a good man—the sort of man who had raised the sort of girl that Juliette was: smart, kind, hardworking, loved.

This was the moment we'd been waiting for, when our perceived enemy was close enough to hear John's voice but not close enough to kill him. Now was the time when they could save their lives, and we could end this senseless war and begin rebuilding our nation. I could tell from the expression on my husband's face that he was praying as John was unfolding the notebook paper from his pocket. I was close enough to see the scribbled lines and crossed-out sentences. There were two authors: one wrote neatly, methodically; another wrote fast and pressured, as if the world depended on her words.

John held the paper as he raised the microphone. He opened his mouth, his eyes reading the paper. He closed his mouth and lowered the paper. His eyes closed for only a moment. He held the paper at his side.

"You matter." He said the words as if he was speaking to someone he loved, not someone who was trying to kill us.

"I'm sorry that we did not do a good job of showing you that before all of this. I'm sorry that you felt unheard and unwanted."

His words bounced across the pavement and between the brick buildings.

"Those feelings of desperation and anger led to this," he said, raising his hands. "Our nation has been attacked. *We* attacked it. No, not literally. None of us here today, regardless of where your weapon is pointed, was actually part of that attack. We all bear responsibility for it, perhaps me more than most because I was in the government. I was an elected official, and though I tried to cross the divide that defined American politics, I didn't try hard enough. I let my own frustrations and anger keep me from remembering that I was in DC to serve, not to demand my own way."

John moved to the front of the picnic table that had been brought from a park and used to hold maps. He sat on top of it.

"Life was hard here in DC, life was hard everywhere in this great country. It was hard because we made it hard. We did it to ourselves. In our excess of material goods, we forgot what actually mattered—civility, kindness, respect, an educated populous. Perhaps some of my colleagues acted like second-rate celebrities because that is what their constituents expected from them." His voice was thoughtful, not blaming.

"No, I don't think that's true. I think it was their pride and my pride. We each believed the lie that, to please those who elected us and keep our job, we must be the loudest, most obnoxious voice in the room. We forgot that a true leader listens far more than he speaks, and sacrifices personal glory for the benefit of those he serves. That's what we forgot. We all forgot we were elected to serve the people, to do what they wanted and needed us to do, and to do it with kindness and civility. When we forgot this, when our nation forgot this, there were some who decided we had reached our end. That our nation had reached her end. We stand now at that end."

He lowered the microphone and rested his voice, watching in the distance as groups of people emerged cautiously from the fringes of the buildings.

He lifted the microphone and said, "It is the end in a lot of ways. I do not know all the names of the loved ones you have lost, but I know the names of mine. I know the sound of their voice, the beauty in their eyes as they laughed at something silly I did. I know these things and they will never be forgotten." He swallowed hard as he rubbed his eyes, taking away the tears.

"But it is the beginning, as well. Those of us who are still alive, we still live in the greatest nation in the world. It is the greatest not because of its military strength—though we do still have much of that—but because of the idea it was founded on. We believed that every person matters, that every person should have a say in how their country is run, and that every person should have the right to life, liberty, and the pursuit of happiness. I still believe those things. I still believe in the hope of democracy. I still believe in the beauty of every man, woman, and child that lives in this great nation."

The crowds stepped closer.

"We have suffered tremendous losses, but we have gained tremendous truths. As a nation we had forgotten the value of sacrifice. It wasn't our fault. We lived in an age of instant gratification and forgot that things worth having take time to earn. Each of us alive now has had that lesson ingrained in our heart and mind. As long as we live, it will never be forgotten.

"Most of you have also learned the great secret that my fellow politicians never wanted you to learn, but we all knew. That truth is that the government can't fix everything. In fact, it can fix very little. The responsibility for your lives falls to each of you. That is scary, and because of that, many people offered up that responsibility out of fear, fear that the world was too hard to change and your life too difficult to manage. And so you craved leaders who would fix it for you and manage it for you. But I assure you,"—he stepped off the picnic table and held his left hand out—"I assure you, you could do a better job than this! Some of you have been told you are slaves." His voice was angry, filled with passion. *"That is a lie!"* his voice boomed. "You are free. Let no one tell you otherwise. I stand before you as a representative of the rightful government of the United States of America. I stand before you as her vice-president, and I can assure you that if you are profiting off the forced labor of children,"—his voice growled—"of women, of men, you will be stopped. And you will be held fully accountable for every single crime you have committed against your fellow citizens and against humanity. Systemic slavery was abolished in this nation over one hundred and fifty years ago and it will never, ever be tolerated again!"

He took a moment to calm his anger. "This attack, which was orchestrated by some of our own citizens, has brought out our worst ..."

I glanced at Richard.

"And our best."

My mind went to the town where Mrs. Pryce and Becca were thriving.

"It is our best that we must take forward. It is our best that we must hold on to and strive to always be. The government is weakened—no, that is a lie—it is barely alive. It will take decades to rebuild, and in that time, much of our military must be prepared to fend off external threats. The internal state of things must be handled by individuals. We must rebuild our towns and our communities. We must begin the process of healing, though how that is possible I do not know, not really. We have all lost"—his voice faltered—"so much. My wife and son were killed. How or why, I don't know, but I feel that they are dead. I can feel them now beside me, just as I am sure you can feel those you love beside you."

My hand tightened around Jonah's.

John cleared his throat. "Somehow, we must forgive. Not for those who killed them, but for our own sake and for that of the country they have left us to care for. For that is what we are. We are caretakers of this beautiful idea, created so long ago by men and women who could never have imagined a world destroyed, not by bullets and arrows, but by an electromagnetic pulse that simply took away our technology. Perhaps—and I do not say this lightly—perhaps we were too dependent on that technology: our food too far away, our understanding of the natural world too distant. Perhaps as we move forward, we could create a world that not only focuses on the inventions of man, but on the creation of God. Perhaps we could live in union with the natural world instead of in conflict with it. Perhaps then we would not be so easy to destroy.

"Forgive me, these are philosophical ramblings. They have no place in our life as it stands at this moment. At this moment we must decide what idea we believe in. Do you believe, as I do, in democracy and in this country as it was created almost two hundred and fifty years ago, or do you believe in something different, in whatever your commanders are telling you to believe in? That is the choice you must make at this moment. I am the vice-president of the United States of America, and on behalf of the president, I welcome each of you to join us in creating our nation anew. A nation where all human life has equal value. A nation that abolished slavery over a hundred and fifty years ago and will never utilize, nor tolerate its use again. A nation that has always been strong and always offered shelter to the weak, the orphaned, the homeless, the countryless. This is our nation. This is what I am fighting for. This is what I invite you to fight for as well."

There was silence, almost unsettling silence. Jonah stood beside me, our backs against the brick wall of a deserted building. Our commanders stood at the edges, waiting for people to surrender or flee or attack.

Seconds turned into minutes.

I jumped when a shot rang out, echoing, as the speech had, through the buildings and across the park.

"They just shot someone who tried to come toward us," Jael announced, after consulting the woman next to her who was watching the approaching armies with binoculars.

"What did you expect!" Richard yelled. "That a heart-tugging speech would fix everything? That they would come to us, telling us how sorry they are for all the evil they've done and forced others to do? These are not nice people. They rule by fear and oppression. They will only stop when they're dead." He went with his weapon toward the barricade.

Jonah stepped in front of him. "Do not start this war."

"You mean the war that's been raging for nine months?" Richard said.

"Stand down. That's an order," Haz commanded.

"I followed orders once before and it made me a murderer," Richard said, his voice calmer, almost apologetic. "This has to end."

He shoved past Jonah, into the open. He lowered his rifle and fired. Then fired again. The other side erupted with an explosion of bullets. Jael and Haz used their bodies as shields to remove John from the front line. Jonah and I dove for cover. East and Haz ran for higher ground. They would act as snipers.

"Give me your gun," Ash shouted above the firing, holding his gun against Richard's temple.

Richard handed him the rifle.

Ash slung it over his shoulder. "Now get out of the way," Ash growled.

Shots continued from all directions. Even if someone wanted to join us, it would be impossible for them to get to us. Richard had destroyed any possibility of a peaceful ending to this siege of our nation's capital. By the end of this day it would be over; the imposters would be gone. There was no doubt as to who would win.

Twenty-Six
BRIA

Far to the south, additional gunfire started. The navy was no longer waiting silently on their ships.

"Come on." Jonah signaled to me as he lowered himself to the ground and crawled behind the short brick wall that had once marked the edge of a well-kept yard. The grass of that yard was as tall as the brick, soft and delicate against my skin.

We were now beside Jael and Ash. Ash had Richard's rifle pointed into a slat in the wall. He fired and then fired again. Jonah did the same and so did I. I didn't want to kill anyone; I aimed at the legs. My first target, a woman, fell to the ground in pain. I turned and fired at my next target. I missed and fired; I got him the second time. I hated what I was doing. I hated killing. Because even though I was only wounding, without surgery or antibiotics those wounds would kill.

The sun was getting lower in the sky. Would this day end with a free nation? There was really no doubt in my mind. There were more of them, but we were better armed and we had the navy. Soon, rebels hiding in the south would be forced to face us. I lay on my back, the short stone wall at my head. It had been built for decoration, but was incredibly effective at keeping bullets from hitting us. All of our troops were equally well positioned. I glanced around and from what I could tell, we'd had no losses, whereas the rebels had dozens down and only a few dozen left. This battle would end soon.

I rolled onto my stomach, lifting the barrel of my gun into the hole in the fence. In the distance there was firing, not at us, but at those we were fighting. I squinted. Blaise and Josh ran onto the battlefield, clearly visible before disappearing behind a statue—a statue that was the only protection that part of the field offered, but was behind the attacking forces.

"What are they doing?" I asked in panic.

"They're way too exposed," Jonah said, the fear evident in his voice.

"They're trying to protect that boy," Jael said, between shots.

"By getting themselves killed!" Ash exclaimed in anger.

Jael was right. There was someone else with them. His head poked out from the base of the statue.

"That's one of the freedom fighters," Jonah said, as the memory of the young boy storming off to sulk in the corner struck me.

"Why is he there?" I asked, though what I really wanted to know was why my best friends followed a hotheaded, impulsive child to the middle of a battlefield.

He was not their child or their best friend; they barely knew him and yet they were risking their lives—the lives I loved as much as my own—to save him.

Ash said, "He must've gone rogue and they're trying to protect him."

"They need to stop shooting," Jael yelled in anger. "She's too good a shot. People are starting to notice."

She was right. The troops we were fighting started to turn and focus their attention on the statue that was protecting Blaise and Josh. Bullets bounced off the bronze, chunks of concrete flying off the base.

I fired over and over, taking down as many people as I could, no longer caring where I hit them or if they lived or died. Blaise and Josh had to live.

A few soldiers aimed at us, but we were protected; they couldn't hit us and they knew it. They returned their aim to the statue. My heart jumping into my throat, I pulled the trigger over and over until at last there was nothing left to fire. My hands shook and fumbled as I reloaded, terrified to watch Blaise and Josh take the fire, terrified not to.

I began shooting, pulling the trigger again and again. Fear kept me from hitting my targets, fear blurred my eyes and made my hands shake. So many were firing at my friends. I could see enough of Blaise and Josh to know they were using their bodies as shields for the boy, their backs pressed against one another, and he was between their feet.

Their attackers fell one after the other.

More seemed to come. Many that had been focused on us were now turning to them. In the distance, Richard ran forward screaming, jumping onto one of the soldiers, stripping him of his gun, running heedlessly into the open.

"He's trying to draw their fire," Ash said.

Jonah nodded, his aim remaining steady as he took down another of the rebel soldiers.

Richard cried out. He'd been hit in the leg. He fell to his knees, but continued shooting and screaming. He continued to draw their fire. This was what he wanted. He wanted to sacrifice his life for his daughter's.

"Dad," Blaise yelled, stepping out of the shadow of the bronze statue. She would not allow this sacrifice.

"No," I yelled, standing to go to her—Jonah pulled me down onto the long grass as bullets whizzed by us.

"Let me up," I said, fighting against him.

"I go first," he commanded.

I couldn't allow this. I wiggled free of him and made my way back to the stone wall.

"Blaise, no!" Felicia yelled, entering from the side of the battlefield, the same side her daughter and son-in-law had entered from. She ran, firing at those closest to her daughter. Two of them fell.

There were so few left, so few still firing. But it didn't matter. Blaise's body jerked. Josh was there to catch her as she fell. She wrapped her arms around him. I jumped over the wall and sprinted toward them, tears streaming. Jonah ran beside me. Jael and Ash beside him. Each of them shooting. So few left, so few enemies. It didn't matter.

Josh's body fell forward and backward, his arms never loosening. He cradled her as the bullets entered both their bodies. His arms never stopped holding her as the life within each of them, the life they gave to each other, ended.

"No, no, no!" I cried.

My body was thrown to the ground, the hard asphalt assaulting any skin it could reach. Jonah was on top of me, holding me down.

"You will not follow them, not today," he said, his voice sorrowful.

Sobs shook my being, my eyes closed tight. Guns near me erupted and then, silence. Silence broken only by loud, convulsive gasps. My sobbing.

Jonah cautiously pulled himself from me. East slid on the pavement beside us, her hands going first to Jonah and then to me. She was speaking, yelling at me, but I didn't hear her. I couldn't hear anything; not because my ears didn't work, but because my mind didn't. I crawled to

Blaise and Josh, hands and knees becoming soaked in blood as I neared them.

Felicia was there, cradling Blaise's head in her lap, her body rocked by convulsive weeping.

Richard crawled, as I did, to his daughter, but behind him a stream of blood fell to the pavement.

I reached them. Fingers shaking, I touched their skin. East appeared. She was doing CPR, tears coursing down her cheeks. Beside her, Haz closed Josh's eyes and then pulled East from Blaise. East held on to him, sobbing.

The images blurred with memories. Memories of the day Blaise met Josh, of his goofy smile, and the flowers he brought to her on their first date. Of her in my mother's wedding dress, of his words promising to be beside her always.

"You kept your promise," I said, touching their clasped hands with my shaking fingers. Already the life was draining, already their bodies were becoming cold. "You were by her side always."

"He will be by her side for eternity," Eli said.

I looked up. I hadn't realized he was there. He knelt between my friends. Jonah stood beside him, East holding him as he sobbed. The sun was gone. When had the sun left us?

The world was in slow motion. My mind wanted to flee, to escape this moment. Was this how Sara felt when her mother died? Was this how her mind broke?

In front of me, Felicia cradled her daughter's head and Richard lay sobbing against her chest. Ash lovingly wiped the blood from Josh's face.

I blinked. Josh's expression was one of peace and joy. I never saw the old man and old woman that Jonah said lay in the house we spent a night in, but he said they looked peaceful. Is that what he meant? Is this what death could be?

"They are at peace now," Eli said. He was speaking to me. He was telling the truth.

Her face was the same as his: there was no pain, there was only peace. They died in each other's arms, just as they lived. They would spend eternity the same way. They loved one another and they loved God. They were at peace in a place where the wars of this world no longer existed.

"Yes," I said, the word sounding strange from my lips.

Eli placed his hands on both of their foreheads, his tears falling, lips moving in silent prayer. In the distance stood the children who were not children, but fighters. They did not cry. They'd experienced too much pain in their young lives to cry over the death of two people they barely knew.

I did not fault them for this.

The salt from my tears entered my lips as I spoke. "I will cry a million tears, but not for you …,"—I inhaled, trying to slow the sobs—"because you're happy and you're safe." I choked. "The tears will be for me and for Sara, because now we have to live in a world without you. You two were what made me believe. Believe in good and the possibility of God."

I knelt forward. "I could see him in both of you," I whispered as I bent and kissed Josh on the forehead and then Blaise on the cheek. "Thank you," I said softly, my tears falling onto her blood-splattered skin. "Thank you for loving me when I couldn't love myself."

Twenty-Seven
BRIA

We flew over the trees in silence. We were nearing home. I'd hoped I'd be able to feel some element of happiness, but I couldn't. I was not foolish enough to believe I would never feel happiness again … time heals wounds. This I learned as a child—though I also learned it did not do its job quickly or without great effort on the part of the person lost in grief.

When the president learned what happened, she graciously allowed us to use two helicopters: the first to transport the living, the second to transport the dead.

I wanted to ride in the second helicopter, to be near Blaise and Josh, but Jonah guided me to the other one. When I turned my eyes to his he told me Eli would ride with them. He would protect them; it would be okay. I'd nodded or somehow agreed and stepped onto the helicopter for the living.

The flight wasn't long, two hours or so. Not a word had been spoken, except between East and the pilot as she guided us home.

John sat across from me. I felt bad for him. He was forced to sit there as stoic as a statue, even though he was about to see his daughter again. But how could he be any different, with Felicia beside him and Richard beside her. And me across.

I leaned against Jonah's chest; he held an arm around me. He'd tried to talk to me a time or two, but I wasn't able to respond. Though I did hear him, the words made little sense. Nothing made sense. Somehow, before we landed, things would have to start making sense again. Sara would be there, and I would not hide from my responsibility. I would be the one to tell her our best friends were no longer part of this world.

The helicopters hovered above the open space between the barn and the house, where both Blaise and I had gotten married.

Beneath us Quint, Heath, and Charlotte pointed guns. Thank God we weren't a threat; they would not have been able to stop us. East allowed the torn cloth to fall from the window. Charlotte cautiously went to it, picking it up, reading the words Jonah had scribbled on it.

The light shines in the darkness, the darkness has never put it out.

The scene below changed in an instant. They lowered their guns. JP, Quinn, and Nonie emerged from the barn, jumping and waving in excitement as the helicopters landed.

East was the first out.

Her parents ran to her so fast and hugged her so hard she would've fallen had Haz not been there to steady all of them. In spite of my pain I smiled at their love, their joy. I glanced at Felicia and Richard. She did not watch the scene; he did, but he did not smile. I felt drawn to them, maybe because I understood their grief was more than mine, because their love for their daughter was more than my love for my friends, though I loved as deeply as I could.

Jonah helped me from the helicopter, leading me across the yard, away from the machines. As we neared his parents and grandmother, he released my hand and went to them. Eli was now out of the second helicopter. He went to his parents. In that moment Charlotte and Quint were surrounded by all of their children. East held Quinn, introducing her to Haz. Even in this time of sorrow it was a moment of joy.

"Where's Juliette?" John asked anxiously.

I turned to him and forced the words to come. "She's around," I answered slowly. "Others are missing too."

I was grateful for that. Grateful Sara was not here waiting for Blaise and Josh to climb from the helicopter.

JP wiggled free from his family and came to me. He hugged me with unexpected strength. "Promise, no more leaving," he said as he squeezed me.

I held him to me, so very grateful to feel his love and strength. So very grateful he was alive. "You've gotten stronger," I said as he constricted his arms against my ribs.

"Promise, or I won't let you go," he said.

"I never want to leave again," I said, and his arms loosened.

This was not what he wanted to hear, but it was all I could give. Things were changing in the world. I had no desire to leave, but life had a way of asking us to do things we had never planned on doing.

My tears formed as Sage and my father emerged from the house, holding hands. At first they were tears of relief—my father was alive—but they soon mixed with tears of sorrow. He was not dead, but he was not far from it. Sage appeared unchanged, her belly no larger than a few weeks ago. My father was the opposite, even more emaciated than when I left. Sage led my father to me. JP released me. I swallowed hard.

Sage gave me a hug but said nothing. She saw the pain in my eyes and left us alone.

"Hi, Dad," I said, kissing him on his cheek, afraid that if I hugged him I would hurt him.

"Bria," he said, weeping. "I didn't think …."

He didn't think he would see me again; he thought he would be dead long before I made it home. These were the thoughts we shared in silence.

"I love you, Dad," I said, taking his hand. His other hand held the cane Quint had made for him months ago.

"I love you too," he said, squeezing my hand.

Silently, JP came and set a stool behind my father.

"Thank you," he said, his voice quiet and raspy. "I'm going to sit," he said to me as he began to lower his body.

JP stood behind him, his hands open, ready to catch my father if he fell. Had he fallen before? Is that why JP knew to do this?

Once my father was settled, JP left and returned with a tree stump. He gestured for me to sit and I did.

"How are you feeling?" I asked my father. In the silence of my heart I wondered how much time I had with him. Had I returned just in time to say goodbye?

He took my hand in his. The bones in his hand felt so frail.

"I'm not feeling well," he said, as tears began to form.

And I understood that the biggest change between now and when I left him was not the time that had passed, but the truth he had accepted. With me gone, he didn't need to pretend to be okay; he was free to allow his body to collapse, and he had. He had given up. No, I thought, that wasn't fair. That made it seem as though he had a choice.

"It's okay, Dad," I said, holding his hand with both of mine.

"I'm sorry you have to see me like this. I'd hoped …."

I lowered my head and then raised it, choosing to ignore what he left unsaid, that he'd hoped to be dead before I came back.

"You're as handsome as ever," I said.

"Even as a child, you were a horrible liar," he said, his voice weak and tired.

"I knew you were sick," I said. "I was afraid I would come back and you wouldn't be here. It's a gift for us to be together now."

"I'm a burden," he said.

I paused, wondering how much to share. "When we were in DC we went to your apartment," I said, deciding to tell him the truth. "It had been ransacked."

"That doesn't matter," my dad responded. "Nothing there matters."

"No, it doesn't," I said, agreeing. "What we shared before wasn't a life. We weren't a family."

My father did not flinch or react in any way to my words; I was grateful for that. I wasn't trying to hurt him, only to be honest with him. "Since you came back to me, we haven't had a lot of time together. This time we've been given now is a gift."

"I don't want to take from you," he said. "I took so much from you when you were a child, I don't want to take more."

I held his hands. "A lot was taken from you too. Maybe somehow this is a gift to you. Your body is sicker," I said, "but *you* are healthier. Whatever time we have is time I didn't think would ever exist. Going back to that apartment reminded me of who we were back then. I never thought any of this could happen—not the ending of the world as we knew it—but the healing of our family."

"Healing did seem far less likely than the world ending," he said with fatigue.

"This moment is a gift and every moment I have with you I will treasure."

"You are so much like your mother," he said, touching my face with his leathery fingers.

Dirt flew around us as the helicopter that had carried us here took off. I tucked my head into my arm. Once the helicopter was gone, I lifted my gaze and my father did the same. His attention went, as mine did, to the second helicopter, the one still on the ground, that held Blaise and Josh.

"What happened?" he asked, with horror in his voice.

Felicia was near the helicopter, being held by Charlotte and Maria. All were crying. Richard was off to the side as Eli and Jonah disappeared into the helicopter and then carried Josh's body, covered in a thin white sheet, out to the yard.

East left Sage's side, handing a crying Quinn to her. East went silently with Haz into the helicopter. They returned, gently carrying Blaise's body. Felicia crumbled. The women around her tried but failed to lift her. Her sadness was too heavy.

The yard was silent as my friends were carried and placed on a spot of soft grass. John closed the helicopter door and the blades began to spin. Jonah and Eli held the sheets over my friends as the second helicopter lifted and disappeared into the afternoon sky.

Both helicopters would return to DC. One would be back in a week to take John, Juliette, and Haz back to DC. That was the deal. John had been allowed to stay only because Haz swore to protect him, even if it meant sacrificing his own life. However, no one, including the president, believed he was in danger at our home. Despite the harvesters coming closer, this area of the country was, for the most part, peaceful.

"Is that Blaise and Josh?" my dad asked, the words so quiet and pain filled they were barely audible.

I squeezed his hand and said nothing as I stared at the sheets. My tears fell nonstop. JP was hugging Quinn, and Sage's arms circled both of them, all of them crying. Charlotte, Nonie, and Quint knelt beside Josh and Blaise. Charlotte carefully pulled the sheet back from Josh's forehead and kissed it as her body shook with sobs. Nonie's wrinkled hand rested against his hair, her thumb making a cross on his forehead. Quint knelt behind them, his face contorted in pain. Nonie lifted the sheet from Blaise's face, and Felicia cried out as if in physical pain. Richard was beside her, holding her.

My father's hand went to my back; the gesture brought forth fresh tears.

"The battle was almost over," I said, snot and tears mixing on my lip. "A boy ran out of their hiding place. He thought he saw his dad. The dad who left him when he was a baby. It wasn't him. Blaise and Josh followed the boy onto the battle field. They saved him."

My father's expression exuded the pain he felt, the pain we all felt. "I'm so sorry," he whispered.

In the distance, Felicia pushed Richard away and ran into the woods. My heart broke for Blaise. I hoped she was too busy in heaven to notice her parents were falling apart.

Charlotte stood, squeezed Quint's shoulder, and followed her.

Quint went toward Richard. Richard held up a hand to stop him, and limped away in the other direction. Jonah came toward us. John followed. Eli and East sat beside the bodies of my dead friends.

When Jonah came beside me, I stood and hugged him, relishing the feel of his arms around my body. The life that pulsed inside him gave me strength when I had none. As much as I mourned Blaise and Josh, their dying together was a gift. It is what they would have wanted, and that awareness brought me some amount of peace.

John stood nearby.

"You've been very patient," Jonah said to him as his arms loosened around me.

"It feels wrong to be happy when there is such tragedy, but please, do you know where Juliette is?" he asked, addressing my dad.

"I believe I heard talk of her and Sara going hunting," Dad answered.

"Hunting?" John asked, sounding surprised. How much his daughter had changed!

Jonah said, "She's one of the best shots we have."

With Blaise gone, she was second only to Richard and maybe Quint.

John was quiet and so was my father. East and Eli went toward the barn. A moment later they returned, each carrying a shovel. I closed my eyes as my head leaned against Jonah's chest.

"Is she your child?" my dad said.

I raised my head as he gazed at John, who had a slight smile on his lips.

"How did you know?" John said.

"You have her eyes," Dad said, the thick lines around his eyes growing deep. "They usually hunt to the west. The stream is a bit wider up there and the animals seem to like that."

"Thank you!" John exclaimed. He abruptly turned as if he were going to search for her.

"Though," Dad said thoughtfully, "I expect those helicopters will have them coming back here any minute. If I were them, I'd be terrified, wondering what was happening here after those birds landed and took off."

John stopped mid stride. "Yes, that makes sense," he said reluctantly.

"Are they on the horses?" Jonah asked, and I realized Fulton and Talin hadn't come to greet us.

Dad nodded. "They did that the other day. Used the horses to go a good ways, then leave them and go the rest of the way on foot. It lets them hunt from farther away, hopefully leaving other animals closer in case we need them in the winter."

"Juliette knows how to ride?" John asked.

"Juliette can do anything she decides to do. She's an impressive young woman," Dad answered, his voice growing stronger at the mention of her name.

Jonah kissed the top of my head. "I'm sorry," he whispered, "the others need my help."

I moved my head from his shoulder and released my arms from around his waist. He kissed me gently on the cheek and my hand remained in his.

Eli, East, and Haz were making their way toward the front of the house, carrying the shovels. They would go to our cemetery to dig the graves for Blaise and Josh.

I allowed my hand to fall from Jonah's. In the woods I detected movement. "Who's there?" I asked, pointing for him to see.

Jonah said, "The horses and riders have returned."

Juliette and Sara were cautiously stepping from the trees, Fulton and Talin behind them.

My emotions overflowed: joy at the thought of Juliette and John being reunited, relief that Talin and Fulton were okay, and dread that Sara would soon learn of our loss.

John jumped up and began to run. "Juliette," he called out.

She stood still as a statue, watching him approach. As he got closer, her posture changed. She recognized him and began running with all her force to him. Juliette jumped into his arms, and he held her, twirling her around and around, and finally came to a wobbly stop. He set her on the ground and dropped to his knees in front of her.

Sara was watching them.

"I'll be back, Dad," I said as Jonah and I went to Sara, grateful she hadn't looked beyond Juliette and John. Grateful she hadn't seen our dead friends.

"You're alive!" Juliette said, holding her father's face in her hands and peering into his crying eyes.

He nodded.

"And you found me," she said in disbelief. "I never thought I'd see you again."

"Your mom and brother?" John asked.

Jonah and I stood motionless, waiting anxiously for her to answer the question we already knew the answer to.

Juliette's face changed, her expression turning pained as she shifted her eyes from her father. She returned her gaze to him, closed her eyes, and shook her head as tears fell from her young face.

John stood and pulled her to him, his head resting on hers as he cried silently, keeping his body strong and stable for his daughter. He had mourned their loss a million moments before this one, but he had hoped. That hope brought him his daughter, but it could not bring him his wife and son, not in this life.

He stopped his tears; he had the rest of his life to mourn.

"You've grown," he said, and then sniffed.

"She should have. She eats more than me," Sara teased kindly.

Everyone laughed, including Juliette. It was the truth.

"I can't believe you found Juliette's dad!" Sara said, excitedly hugging first me and then Jonah.

My voice was too weak to speak.

Jonah answered. "It was Haz and East who found him."

"Are they here?" Her eyes were wide and bright, filled with joyous anticipation.

Juliette's expression matched hers.

"Yes," Jonah answered. "Everyone is here." His voice faltered only slightly.

Juliette stood on her tiptoes, looking into the distance, around Jonah and me. Her expression changed drastically and she clung tighter to her father. He understood and held her, protecting her as best he could from feeling the pain of this moment.

Sara's eyes grew wide with panic as she stared first at the sheets and then at me.

"Blaise and Josh," I said through renewed tears. These were for Sara … for her loss and her sorrow.

She stared in disbelief, her hand going to her mouth as she stepped past us. We followed. I released Jonah and went to her.

"How?" she asked as she forced her legs forward.

"There was a battle," I said. "They saved a boy."

I was grateful for that last part, grateful I could say they offered their lives to save another. It's how they would choose to die; it *was* how they chose to die.

Sara fell, kneeling beside our friends. I followed her to the soft earth. Eli came beside us. He took her hand in his.

"They didn't suffer," he said to her.

She nodded.

"I'm sorry," I said, through tears. "I'm so sorry I couldn't save them."

Sara held on to me and I to her as we cried until neither of us could cry any longer.

"They're together," she said, the tears falling into her slightly upturned mouth.

"Y-yes." I sniffed. "It's how they always were."

"They've left us," she said, weeping.

A sob escaped me before I could stop it. "They will be waiting for us."

She held me as new tears flowed.

Twenty-Eight
BRIA

Thunder escaped from the dark clouds above us. Only Jonah, Sara, and I remained; the others had left slowly, one after another, to return to the house. Jonah stayed to finish filling in the grave Blaise and Josh now shared. Sara and I stayed because we couldn't leave.

After placing the last shovelful of dirt, Jonah wiped his forehead with his arm. This action replaced the sweat of his forehead with the dirt of his arm, but it didn't matter; the rain would wash it away soon enough.

"Do you think the rain is Blaise's way of telling us to get up and get on with our lives?" Sara said from beside me.

"That does sound like Blaise," I said.

Jonah stepped away from the graves and stuck the shovel into the ground. He came toward us. "It's time to go," he said, reaching his dirt-encrusted hands toward us. We each took one and he stepped backward, pulling us up.

I wiped the dirt from the seat of my pants. Sara did the same. We stared at the grave, marked by two simple wooden crosses, as we'd been doing for the last several hours.

The rain increased as Jonah pulled the shovel from the earth and started up the path toward the houses. Sara and I stood there, arm in arm.

"They are telling us to go," Sara whispered.

"Yes," I said, my hair beginning to stick to my scalp. "But I don't want to."

Watching Haz and Jonah place them one after the other into the grave had made my chest feel as if it was going to collapse. Listening to Eli speak of the love they shared, the life they created, brought new tears. Feeling the dirt between my fingers as I scooped a symbolic handful onto their sheet-lined bodies left me empty, as if I had given part of my soul to them. Eli said that's what it was like to love. To give part of yourself to someone else. My best friends.

Felicia's pain reminded me that as much as I loved, I did not love like a mother loved. From Richard, I felt love, but I also felt anger and hatred. I wasn't sure who those emotions were aimed at. I wanted to tell him not to do what my father had done. Don't waste your life. Don't push away those who love and need you. But I didn't have the courage.

Instead I watched as Felicia reached for him and he allowed her to take his hand. But he had not offered it. I hoped she would never stop reaching for him, but I knew that everyone eventually comes to the end of their strength and she was not far from that point.

"Don't stay much longer," Jonah said, the rain dripping from his hair. He walked through the tall summer grasses mixed with wildflowers, the gift he and his mother had given my mother and brother so many years before.

"How will we go through life without them?" I asked, the falling rain somehow bringing me hope as it soothed my cracked lips and rinsed the salt from my cheeks.

"Have you ever listened to the end of the rosary?" Sara asked as our shoes filled with falling water. "The end part that's asking Mary to help us as we go through this valley of tears? I don't know if I would have described life that way before my mom, and Blaise and Josh, but it seems like the right description now."

"Yeah, it does."

Sara knelt and lowered her head. She placed the palms of her hands on the fresh earth. After a few minutes she stood.

"Soon wildflowers will grow in this mud," she said.

She turned to me. "Soon we will be able to be happy again."

"Yes," I said, glancing at the graves of my mother and brother. The area was covered in grass and a few remaining wildflowers holding on to the edge of summer. I looped my arm through Sara's, and we held each other close as we silently left our friends, an unspoken awareness growing between us. We would always be best friends. That would never change, but it would never be like it once was, when the four of us lived our lives together and were each other's family.

We each had our own families now, our own lives, moving forward. I had my father, though that time would not last long, and I had Jonah. I prayed my time with him would last for eternity.

Sara had her sister and the baby that would soon be born. But more than that, she had God. He had become for her what she had tried to make all the boys become. God had become the one her every breath was for. She would remain here for a while, long enough for Sage to have her baby, but then her love would take her away from here. She hadn't spoken this, but with our arms looped I could feel it. She was being called to leave our sanctuary.

It was the same with Eli. He hadn't wanted to leave the freedom fighters. We all felt the fighters needed someone to care for them and all the others like them, but only Eli was sure it had to be him.

Sara did not know the freedom fighters and the others who I was sure would someday find her. She did not know they would be the ones she would spend her life caring for, but I did.

We stepped onto the wider path. Jonah was up ahead, his head bent low to keep the rain from falling in his eyes.

"He's moving slow, waiting for you," Sara said.

I laughed, and it didn't feel wrong to do so. It felt as if Blaise and Josh were laughing beside me.

"What is it?" Sara asked.

"I heard Josh's voice making fun of me, saying 'Yeah, that poor guy has spent his life waiting for her to catch up.'"

Sara held on tighter. "That sounds like him."

The wet stones crunched beneath our slippery feet, and without the protection of the trees, the rain fell harder. We lowered our heads as Jonah had done, to protect our eyes. Water ran in narrow streams down the road created more than a century before, to connect my ancestors' home to the rest of the world.

I said, "I wonder what it will be like, now that there is peace in DC."

"The world will grow again," Sara answered. "We will no longer be confined to the pockets of safety we've created. We will be able to go beyond those boundaries."

"The thought of that scares me," I said honestly.

"There are moments it scares me too, but there are times in human history when people must retreat into themselves, leaving the outside world to do as it will, and there are times when people must go out and shape the world with courage and conviction."

As I felt the rain pelting my skin, I became vaguely aware that she was no longer speaking about the world as I saw it, but the world as she saw it—the world where people's physical life was important and their spiritual life was far more so.

"I don't feel that courage and conviction," I answered.

"Then it is not your time," she said simply.

No, I thought it is not my time to leave this place; it was my time to stay. It was my time to be a daughter and a wife and at the same time learn who I was, independent of everyone else.

Jonah had disappeared into the barn. I slowed my pace and Sara slowed hers to match.

"My dad is dying," I said, thinking of my father. Too weak to walk to the funeral, he'd instead been carried atop Fulton. JP held the reins and Quint walked beside him to ensure he didn't fall off.

Sara hesitated. "Yes, I know."

We stood together in the falling rain.

She held my arm with both of her hands. "It's his time," she said.

A tear escaped, covered by the rain, "Yes," I said.

Sara released her hold on me as Jonah neared, shovel no longer in hand. The dirt was washed away, his hair and clothes dripping.

Sara leaned forward, kissing me on the side of the face. She looked lovingly at me and then at Jonah. She pulled her hair back, the curls still strong despite the heavy rains. She stepped onto the doorstep and went into the house, the warm firelight escaping when she entered.

I leaned into Jonah, his arms going around me.

"How are you?" he asked.

I shrugged, my shoulders moving against his body. "They would want me to be happy, to move on with life."

"Yes," Jonah said, "but if they were the ones left behind and we were dead, it would not be easy for them to do, either."

I held him. "I love you," I said, grateful our life together was not ending, but just beginning.

He bent his head to mine, our lips touching, the soft water falling on us, washing away the tears and dirt and pain of the past.

"I love you too," he said. He gently pushed a wet strand of hair behind my ear. "Can we go in now?" he said, with the smallest hint of a smile. "The rain is cold."

"Is it?" I said, blinking up at him.

He kissed my lips again. "That's one of the many things I love about you. You feel so deeply you forget to be cold."

He took my hand and led me through the doorway, the warmth instantly replenishing me.

Twenty-Nine
EAST

Every living person I loved was in the same room. Funerals had a way of doing that, of pulling together loved ones who understood how precious that moment was. Bria and Jonah were the last to enter and were drenched. It reminded me of the first night we came to this place, the first night I realized my brother was helplessly in love with a girl who had no idea who she was. So much had changed since that night.

Now they sat beside one another in front of the fire, no longer hiding from themselves or each other. The more they loved one another, the more they had become themselves. This is what love was supposed to be. It was supposed to bring out your best as you worked to support and uplift the other. This is what it had done for my brother and Bria, for my parents and grandparents before them, even Blaise and Josh had achieved this. I wondered if at one point Blaise's parents had also had this type of love.

No one told Haz and me the specifics of what happened to Richard and Felicia, but enough had been spoken and more implied that something terrible had been done. They sat beside one another, but were less connected than even Haz and I were. If I allowed it to, my heart would ache for them, but I would not allow it—not yet.

The battle was over. Maybe the war was also, but it was too soon to know. It was too soon to feel as much as my true self wanted to feel. I could not be like Sara and Bria.

They were huddled beside each other, each grieving the loss of best friends that were far more like family. It was in Holt's apartment that I got a glimpse of what Bria's life before all of this was like. And because of that glimpse I accepted what she said the day we decided to leave here, the day Sara fixed that old truck. Holt may have provided for her physical needs, but not emotional and certainly not spiritual. It was Blaise, Sara, and Josh who had taught Bria what it meant to be part of a family. And now she would be forced to exist without two who loved her and whom she loved. I was sorry for her, sorry for all of us.

Death is common now. People have to accept it and continue on with life.

Bria would soon lose her father. Dad said it was cancer, or at least that was his guess. I was there when John offered to take Holt back to DC. Dr. Mudd and others were there, along with some technology that might extend his life. Holt thanked him, but refused. I didn't blame him; no one did. He was ready to be with his wife and son.

Bria would be all right without him. He knew that and so did she. She would miss him terribly, but, as with Blaise and Josh, she would accept the loss and move on. She had become strong and resilient, so different from the spoiled girl we'd met on the side of the road last Thanksgiving. The only one she could not live without was Jonah, and he was no different. If it had been Bria shot by those troops, Jonah would have done exactly as Josh did: gone to her and happily welcomed death as he held her dying body.

Haz nudged me with his shoulder. "I'm going to get some blackberry pie. Would you like some?"

"Yes," I answered as he pushed himself off the ledge of the countertop.

I handed him my plate. "Be right back," he said as he went toward the food.

My mother was watching me watch him. I lowered my eyes. My feelings for him didn't matter. He would be leaving in a few days, when the helicopter returned for John and Juliette, and would not return for at least six months. That was the agreement Juliette made with her dad. She would go with him, but she wanted to come back to meet Sage's baby and bring us one of Astrea's puppies. He happily agreed. They would return in the spring. Hopefully, the snow would be melted and Sage would have her baby. Juliette was almost as excited about the baby as Nonie, so there was no doubt she would return. The only real question was would Haz be with her.

"Here you go," he said, handing me the pie.

"Thank you," I said, taking it from him, our hands touching, and in the process a shiver ran through my body.

"Anything for you," he said, standing beside me rather than sitting on the counter.

"It's just pie," I said, taking a bite.

He tilted his head, his dimples coming to life. "Sometimes when a man does something nice for a woman, it means more than the simple act he has performed."

"And sometimes a piece of pie is just a piece of pie," I said, and took another bite.

I saw the smile in his eyes.

"Nobody," he said. "There is nobody else on the planet like you."

"That's a good thing," Jonah said as he brushed past us on his way to the food.

"I agree," Haz said, never taking his eyes from mine.

Heat was rising to my cheeks, but I refused to blush.

"Oh, I forgot!" JP exclaimed, and ran from the room.

Mom said, "What was that about?"

"What is it ever about?" Dad answered as Mom leaned into him.

"JP is strange," Quinn stated as she shook her head.

"There is a level of strangeness to him," Eli said, "but it's endearing."

"Maybe to you!" Quinn shouted.

The door sprang open and JP ran in, out of breath. He went to Bria. "I … found … this … yesterday," he said, panting. "I didn't … want anyone … to eat it." He unwrapped the cloth in his hands, revealing a bright red apple.

"The first ripe apple?" Bria said with wonder.

He nodded excitedly. "You made it back," he said, with the excited energy of the boy he was before life had become so hard.

Bria stood and hugged him. He returned the hug, but it was the kind that is part hug and part "let me show you my strength as I try to squeeze the life out of you." Bria coughed and he released her.

"Will you share it with me?" she asked him.

"I thought we could cut it up and everyone could have some," JP said, proud of his contribution to the meal.

"Great idea," Mom said, taking the apple to the cutting board. She cut it into thin slivers and handed the board to JP. He proudly stepped around to each of us.

I took two pieces, one for me and one for Haz. "In case you're wondering, this is just an apple, no hidden meanings or anything," I said, teasing him.

"I don't know," Haz responded. "It seemed to have a meaning for Bria and your little brother."

"All right, there was a hidden meaning for them, but for the rest of us it's just an apple," I said, biting into my piece.

"This is the best apple I've ever eaten," Bria said in a gush as JP returned to her side. She placed an arm around him.

"I knew it would be," JP answered as he nibbled around the core.

"I wish there was more," Quinn said after she finished her sliver.

"The trees are full," Dad answered. "A few more days and you'll be able to eat all the apples you want."

"And a few days after that you'll be sick of apples," Mom joked as she lifted Quinn.

"I'll never be sick of apples. They're my favorite," Quinn answered, snuggling into Mom's neck.

"Your daughter is beautiful," Haz whispered, so quietly that for a moment I wondered if I'd heard the words or imagined them, my own thoughts so loud they might have become words.

I turned to him, holding his gaze longer than I meant to.

"Yes," I said, finally blinking, my voice as quiet as his. "She is."

Six Years Later

The sun was bright, the day hot as I knelt between my parents' graves. My infant son slept against my chest, tied in the way Nonie had taught first Sage and, later, me, to wrap our babies against us. I used the rag in my hand to rub the dirt from my mother's and brother's polished stones. My father's was the same type as the one Blaise and Josh shared, a smooth unpolished stone with their names and dates lovingly carved into it. The unevenness of these stones made them more difficult to clean.

My daughter Faustina ran to me, silently placing the wildflowers she and her cousin Hope had picked, onto my father's grave.

"Thank you, sweetie," I whispered as she precisely placed each delicate flower on her grandfather's grave.

Faustina had never met her grandfather, yet she loved him deeply. The love came from the stories I told her. Of how he loved more than any person ever, so much so that when Grandma and Uncle Holt died, Grandpa's heart turned to stone from the sadness. But after many years, he allowed God to heal his hardened heart and Grandpa began to love again. It was because of that love that he walked in the deep snow for days and weeks to find Mommy. This is how he saved Mommy and Daddy and Grammy and Grampy and everyone else.

"He was so brave," she would always whisper.

"Yes," I would say, "and you are just like him."

How different she and I were. She was connected to her past, whereas I had been ripped from mine. The truth of that statement brought me peace. Her life was nothing like mine; her early choices would be nothing like mine. I hoped her later choices would be the same as mine. I hoped she would marry a man as good as her father and love as deeply as I loved her, her brother, and Jonah. This, I decided, made life worth all the suffering. Jonah still said the point of life was to know God, love God, and serve God, and I now agreed, but to me that was best done in knowing my children and husband, in loving them, and in sacrificing for them.

My father's illness had lasted only a few months after we returned home. He was gone before Haz, Juliette, and John returned that April. I was grateful for the time I had with him. Grateful I could care for him as my mother would have wanted me to.

Jonah was beside me when my dad died, his hand in mine as the suffering finally came to an end. It was in that moment that I saw Christ. In my father's ravaged body, I saw the total offering of Christ's crucified body, and on Dad's face there was redemption. A peacefulness came as he slipped from this world. His pain was gone, his heart was whole. He was with my mom and brother and our Savior. In the end it was his witness, more than anyone else's, that brought me back to the faith of my birth.

The phone in my back pocket buzzed. I pulled it out and clicked off the alarm.

"Three more minutes, girls," I said.

They quickened their pace of gathering flowers and I quickened mine.

I moved to the stone marking Blaise and Josh's grave. Tears filled my eyes. They always did.

"Your Auntie Blaise and Uncle Josh love you so much," I said to Joshua, whose eyes were now open and staring up at me.

I rubbed the dirt from their stone and sniffed my tears. "You would have loved them. Just like I did," I said, my arms wrapping around him.

From behind me I heard the horses. I kissed my fingers and placed them on the stone on top of Blaise's name. I rocked up onto my feet just as Jonah, Fulton, and Talin entered the meadow.

"Your daddy's right on time," I said as Joshua and I went to him.

Faustina ran, arms open, and leapt into Jonah's arms. He lifted her. "Are you ready to go see Grammy and Grampy and your aunties?"

"Mmm-hmm," she said, nodding her head, her green eyes, the color of sea glass, bright with excitement.

Jonah gave me a soft kiss and placed his hand lightly on Joshua's head. "How has your morning been?" he asked.

"Nothing eventful, so, good," I said, as Hope joined us.

"Well, all that's about to change," he said in his excited dad voice. "The helicopter should be here in ten minutes."

The girls squealed and clapped.

"I ride wiff Daddy," Faustina said, clinging to Jonah as she often did.

"Okay then, I get Hope," I said, winking at our niece.

Jonah helped me onto Talin. Joshua cooed with excitement; he loved riding as much as the rest of us did.

"You ready?" Jonah said as he prepared to lift Hope.

"Yes," she said, and in less than a second she was sitting behind me, her little arms wrapping around my belly. She laid her body against mine, and it was in moments like this when I felt how small her body was and remembered she was only six. Her little life was the way I marked time. It was her birth that signaled the end of the fighting, for us and for most of the country.

Pam was now halfway through her second term as president. Power was restored to DC and with the manufacturing of new phones, global communication was restored to many. We had electric lights and refrigeration in the main house, thanks to Sara's windmill, and a working refrigerator in my house, again thanks to Sara's ingenuity, along with some newly manufactured solar panels. During the winters we moved into the main house where it was warmer, but the other nine months of the year the four of us stayed by ourselves in the house my parents had built. Heath and Maria had called this house their own until it was safe enough for them to move back to their own property closer to town.

Talin started forward and Hope tightened her grip around my waist. It was because of Hope that I had the courage to try for a child of my own. Hope was strong and her birth was uncomplicated. She grew as all babies should. Sicknesses came, but she survived. We all did.

A little after Hope's second birthday I told Jonah I was open to kids. True to what he told me the day of our first real kiss, he was ready to move forward in our relationship whenever I was. Children were that next terrifying step.

When Faustina was born my heart felt like it was going to explode; never had I felt love like that. As Jonah held her, my tears came with such force it scared us both. I understood at that moment the loss my father experienced when my mother and brother died. Any past hurt I still held, left at that moment.

Joshua giggled as we bounced up and down on Talin. I tightened my arm around him and inhaled the smell of his baby skin so close to mine. I had been terrified to have him, though not because I was afraid I would die. My pregnancy with Faustina was easy and healthy. Her birth was like Hope's, uncomplicated. No, with Joshua I was afraid I could never love another child as much as I loved Faustina. Jonah confessed he was worried about the same thing.

It was a pointless worry. When Joshua was born it was as if my heart grew. I felt as much love for him as I did Faustina and, though it seemed impossible, my love for her grew. The same happened with my love for Jonah. I thought I loved him on the day we got married. But looking back almost seven years, the love I felt then was like a tiny drop in a swimming pool.

"Don't go too fast," I called as Faustina laughed, Jonah's right arm around her.

"We aren't going fast," Jonah called, offering me his "Don't worry, Momma, I've got this" look, which never did anything to settle my fears, only increase them.

"You don't have to worry," Hope's tiny voice said. "Fulton would never go very fast with Faustina on him."

"You're right," I said, "but I'm a momma and mommas worry."

"Not my momma," Hope said.

"Your momma worries," I said, trying to sound convincing. Sage adored Hope, but Hope came so easy to her she sometimes didn't recognize how fragile she was, how fragile we all are.

"Auntie Bria, don't tell fibs. Momma loves me, but she doesn't worry. It's not in her nature."

"Did Aunt Sara tell you that?" I asked.

She hesitated. "I figured it out myself, but she didn't tell me I was wrong."

"Maybe your mom knows that you already have enough people to worry about you because you have Aunt Sara, and me, and Grammy, Grampy, and Nonie, and, of course, all your big cousins and your uncles."

Hope giggled. "That is a lot of worriers."

"Yes," I said, grateful my explanation made sense to her.

It had been six and a half years since the death of Faith and the betrayal of Hayden and the deaths of Blaise and Josh. It was too much pain too close together. After Hope was born, Sage stopped pretending she was okay. Felicia thought it was postpartum depression and maybe it was, but I saw it differently. I saw the reality of life setting in on someone who spent most of her life desperately trying to hide from it. She was better now, no longer depressed, but not able to be a full parent to Hope. Nonie said it didn't matter, that there were plenty of others who could step in and that was the point of family, anyway. She was right.

We rode around the back of the house. The others were already there waiting for the helicopter. JohnPaul stood ready to take Talin. He looked far more like a man now than a boy, tall and handsome like his brothers. Pain pricked my heart. It would not be long before he got his wish and was allowed to join East and Eli in DC.

"How was BlaiseFaustina this morning?" he asked Hope as he lifted her from Talin. JohnPaul was the only one who called my daughter by her full name, perhaps because he preferred to be called by his full name.

"She was good, not too busy," Hope said, handing her wildflowers to JohnPaul.

He took them and lifted her from Talin.

"Busy. … That's a nice way of saying it," he said as he took my hand and helped Joshua and me down.

"Don't forget you were quite the active child," I said, teasing him. That hyperactive child disappeared completely a few years ago as he grew into the body of a man.

"Ha. You should've seen him when he was her age," Jonah said, lifting Faustina from Talin. "Makes this one look as calm as Joshua."

"Nonie told me you and Eli were just as tiring," Sage said, winking playfully at Jonah.

"And their father was no better," Nonie said, petting little Joshua's head. "And each of them grew to become amazing men. Faustina will grow to be a gift to the world, I have no doubt."

"Isn't everyone a gift to the world?" JohnPaul asked his grandmother.

"Yes, yes, of course," Nonie said. "Though some children, like my grandchildren and great-grandchildren, for instance, have a few more bows on their packages than others." She leaned against the arm he held out for her. Her hands were soft and wrinkled. She rarely did manual labor anymore. Her skin had returned to the color of cream, no longer pink from the sun.

Jonah slid off Fulton as the helicopter emerged in the distance.

"Not even a minute late," JohnPaul said, checking his phone.

Jonah held Faustina with one hand and the reins of the horses with the other. Talin and Fulton remained calm despite the noise and wind of the massive machine landing on our lawn. Astrea's puppy, that had not been a puppy for almost six years, barked as the helicopter touched the grass.

I held my hand up to keep debris from flying onto Joshua's head.

As soon as it touched down and the blades began to slow, the door opened. JohnPaul ran to help his dad, mom,

Sara, and youngest sister from the helicopter. A few moments later it was taking off, and we were giving hugs.

When the noise of the machine was gone and the initial hugs were done, Nonie asked, "How's my newest great-grandbaby?"

"Amazing!" Charlotte said, gushing. "The pictures don't do him justice. Dark hair and skin like his dad and—"

"And bright blue eyes like East," Quint said.

"We have beautiful grandchildren," Charlotte said, lovingly glancing at Quinn, who smiled in return.

Jonah and I exchanged a glimpse.

We wondered if this would be the trip when they told Quinn the truth about her biological parents. She was old enough to understand now and Charlotte told us she thought it was time. They didn't want to do it without East, and so Jonah and I had been praying that if this was the time, that Quinn be filled with understanding, love, and peace. By her expression it had gone well; I sensed no anger at her parents and I'm sure there was none for East. Quinn was loved, she'd always been loved, and her faith, like that of the rest of her family, was strong. It was this faith, this sense of where you fit in the world, that helped keep the ever-encroaching darkness out.

"Grampy gone too long," Faustina said in a chastising tone. He was her favorite.

Quint scooped her up. "A month is a long time, but Grammy and I wanted to be there when your cousin Kolbe was born."

Faustina crossed her arms in a gesture that was meant to show anger, but coming from a three-year-old, even one desperately in need of a nap, it only made us smile.

"She's not impressed, Dad," Jonah said.

"Clearly," he said.

"We've been telling her that the whole time you've been gone," I added.

"She wasn't impressed then, either," Jonah added.

Quint refocused on the toddler in his arms. "Grammy and I are home now and we aren't leaving again for quite a while. But a month really isn't very long at all. It used to take your parents a month just to get to DC. Now, at least, the vice-president lets us use a helicopter. Think how long we would be gone if we had to walk, like your mom and dad did?"

"It wouldn't take long," she said in a whiny voice. "Take me for walk. Nobody walked wiff me."

"Oh, now, I don't believe that," Charlotte said, caressing Faustina's pink cheeks.

"It's true," Faustina said, nodding her head with such force it made my neck hurt just watching her.

"Let Grampy get settled," Quint said, sounding tired, "and I can walk with you this afternoon before dinner. We can see all the animals and the garden, okay?"

"No, now," she said, wiggling free from his arms.

"She needs a nap," Jonah said to me.

"Yes, it's a shame the vice-president didn't take our toddler's nap schedule into account when he allowed our family to use his helicopter," I said with a mischievous grin.

"That *is* a shame," Jonah said, kissing me playfully, Joshua bouncing happily between us.

Faustina was pulling at Quint, jumping up and down, trying to make him move.

"Here, Blaise Faustina, come with me to put up the horses," JohnPaul said. "I'll let you brush them."

She bit her lip, trying to decide. "Okay," she finally said, and the two went to the barn, the horses following them.

"Oh, I've missed her," Sara said, watching her go. "She's so full of life. The children in DC aren't like that."

I looped my arm through hers. "Yes, we want to hear about Eli's ministry, but first, how is East?" We'd gotten updates, thanks to the phones, while they were gone, but they always seemed to be not telling us the whole thing.

"She didn't have it as easy as you two," Charlotte said, her arm around Sage.

Quint said, "It's good she was in DC with Dr. Mudd and a few others."

"A few others?" Nonie said with concern. "You didn't tell us any of that. Is she all right?"

"She's fine, Mom. And Kolbe is healthy and growing," Quint said.

"But it was scary," Charlotte said, trying but failing to keep the fear and sadness from her voice. "I don't know if they can have any more children," Charlotte said tearfully.

"We don't know anything of the sort," Quint said, taking his wife's hand. "All technology is advancing at incredible speeds, including the medical ones. We aren't up to where we were before the attacks, but we aren't too far behind. Another few years, and surgeries that aren't possible now might be an option. But if they don't have another child, they will accept that. They understand how blessed they are."

"How is Haz?" Jonah asked with concern. The two had become almost as close as he and Eli were.

"So strong," Charlotte said, with tears and admiration.

"They are a perfect match for each other," Quint added.

"Thank God he's a patient man," Nonie said. "I can't imagine keeping that good-looking boy waiting for five years without even a kiss!"

"He's a good man," Sara said, "but she's an amazing woman and he was smart to wait for her."

We started toward the house, Jonah and Quint carrying the bags and Hope holding hands with Sara and Sage.

"How is DC?" Jonah asked. "And Eli's ministry?"

"They're both growing together. Eli never stops. The only break he gets is his monthly trip to visit Sebastian and Becca at the orphanage. Of course, even then he is transporting children and works when he gets there," Charlotte said, with both pride and worry.

"How is the orphanage?" I asked. My heart swelled with emotion every time I thought of the children who lived there.

"Doing very well," Quint said. "We took a day trip out to it. The farm is extremely productive, thanks to Gus and the Taits, and the children have no shortage of love and solid education, thanks to the rest of the town."

"Jael and Ash visit from time to time," Sara said thoughtfully. "When they can get away from DC."

"Oh, and this one," Charlotte said in frustration, speaking about Sara. "She was no better than Eli. She never sat the entire time we were in DC."

"There was too much to do," Sara said, turning back to us as she swung hands with Hope.

It would not be long until we lost Sara for good to DC; it was her calling to work beside Eli, helping those in most need. We understood that. Sara stayed here only because she could not bear to leave Sage and Hope. Eventually Sage would say it was time for them to go to DC and then we would lose them all. Or Hope would grow older and Sara would go without them. For now, we only lost her every few months.

"Eli's ministry is like nothing I've read about before," Sara said, her left hand going to the leather pouch she wore around her neck. The pouch that contained what was most precious to her in the world, the Eucharist Eli entrusted her to transport safely to our tabernacle. "His ministry bridges the gap and serves those who are poor, in whatever way that means. Many are literally starving and others are figuratively starving. He helps them both and never judges either one. He's a man created for these times."

"Out of the darkness, saints will rise," Nonie said, her old voice strong and forceful.

Joshua bounced in his wrap.

"Do you see Grammy?" Charlotte cooed, and his face lit up.

I unstrapped him. "Here you go, good boy," I said, handing Joshua to Charlotte. She took him in her arms.

"Oh, you've grown," she said.

Quint laughed. "I think you're just used to holding Kolbe. He was tiny, just like East when she was born."

"No, I would never get my grandbabies confused. Joshua has grown. Here, feel for yourself," she said, passing him to Quint.

"Oh my goodness, you have grown!" Quint exclaimed.

Quinn shook her head. "They were like this the entire time. Every time Kolbe opened his eyes, you would think a statue should be built."

"He was so alert," Charlotte said.

"It was remarkable," Quint echoed.

Quinn shook her head again. "You two as grandparents are nothing like you are as parents."

"That's the truth," Jonah said.

"That's the beauty of being grandparents," Quint said, nuzzling his face to Joshua's. "You don't have to be parents. You get to play and love and hand them back when you're tired or they're cranky."

"Oh my gosh," Quinn said, in mock exasperation. "Come on, Hope. Juliette sent you a gift."

"What is it?" Hope said as she jumped up and down while holding on to Quinn's hand.

"I'll give you a hint. You can eat it," Quinn said as they entered the house.

"Chocolate, I bet it's chocolate," Hope squealed. They disappeared into the kitchen.

"Ooh, I want some," Sage said, picking up her pace and following her daughter.

"Did you tell Quinn?" Nonie asked as the hall door closed behind the others.

"We did," Quint said with a nod.

"How did she take it?" Nonie asked.

"As well as anyone could," Charlotte answered.

"She talked with me a little," Sara said quietly. "She wishes you would've told her sooner, though she understands why you didn't."

"It's a delicate balance," I said, sitting down at the table, with Jonah beside me.

"Yes," Sara said, "and she understands that. It's a lot to take in."

"She asked if we lied to her about anything else," Charlotte said with sorrow.

"Such an upsetting, though expected, question," Quint said.

"We were lying," Charlotte said. "She's not wrong about that."

"I know," Quint said. "It just hurts that she thinks of it like that."

"It's a hurtful topic," Charlotte said, her voice stronger, ready to move on. "But all in all, she's doing very well."

"How's the city?" Nonie asked.

"The city is okay," Quint said, still holding Joshua.

"The country is moving along," Charlotte added. "Pam and John have a plan in place for each region. They are prioritizing solar panels to decentralize the power grid. Some of the houses and buildings away from urban areas didn't lose everything. They just thought they had because there was no power."

"Really?" Jonah asked.

"Yes, there are whole hospitals out west that, once power was supplied, powered right up," Sara said.

"That's incredible," I said.

"A miracle," she countered.

"What about the rest of the world?" Jonah asked.

We all felt guilt over the state of the world, to know that our citizens did this. It was a disgusting feeling.

"Africa is doing the best," Sara said. "They weren't as reliant on machines and electricity, so their losses were the least."

"China and India have been hit the worst," Charlotte said. "The populations in their cities were too great and the ecosystems around them too barren for even a tenth of the urban people to survive."

"The world population is now estimated at 2.5 billion people," Quint said sadly. "We lost close to five billion souls."

We were silent as we took in his words.

"Is the population still declining?" Nonie asked.

Quint sat Joshua onto the table, his hands supporting his chest. "Pam says her statisticians believe it will ultimately settle close to two billion before it begins to rise again," Quint said.

I leaned against Jonah and thought of the many we had lost, not just those we loved, but all the others. I didn't understand how we had been so lucky, how we still had each other and our children.

"What about Felicia and Richard?" Nonie asked, worry in her voice.

"Doing better," Charlotte said. "Richard has volunteered a few times with her at Eli's ministry. She told me those days working together to help others was helping them. She said they have a long way to go and that they both want to get there."

"I'm glad," Nonie said.

"We are too," Quint said.

The outside door opened. JohnPaul was carrying a crying Faustina. "She fell. She didn't get hurt, though. I think she needs a nap," he said, stretching his arms out for Jonah to take her.

Jonah stood and I followed.

"No," she sobbed. "No nap."

Jonah and I exchanged a look. She was past the reasoning point.

"Come on," I said, taking Joshua from Quint. "Sister needs a nap."

"No!" She cried harder as Jonah lifted her from JohnPaul.

Quint put his arm around Charlotte.

"Aren't our grandchildren amazing," she said, snuggling against her husband.

"The most amazing ever," Quint answered happily as Jonah tried but failed to get Faustina to stop crying.

"Maybe she'll fall asleep on the way home," I said.

"Nooo, no nap," Faustina bellowed.

"Just like me, huh?" Jonah said as we made our way to the door.

"Just like you, son," Quint called, laughter in his voice, and in the chaos of the moment I was overwhelmed with peace and love.

I shifted Joshua onto my hip and lifted myself onto my tiptoes, leaning against Jonah, kissing him.

"I love you forever," I said.

He turned, Faustina flailing in his arms. "Always and forever," he said, and kissed me lovingly, with Joshua giggling and Faustina crying between us.

THE END

Author's Note

Thank you for joining me as I escaped into the world of Bria and Jonah and all those they love. They live in a world I hope never comes to pass, but in a way, that I pray happens for each of us. They are strong, courageous, selfless, good, and kind. They are flawed, as we all are, yet incredible, as we all are. I pray we can see the good, the true, and the beautiful in the chaos of each of our lives. Thank you from the bottom of my heart for being a part of this incredible journey!

Also by Jacqueline Brown
The Light, Book One of The Light Series
Through the Ashes, Book Two of The Light Series
From the Shadows, Book Three of The Light Series
Into the Embers, Book Four of The Light Series
"Before the Silence," a Light Series Short Story
Awakening

To receive your FREE copy of "Before the Silence," please join the mailing list, or visit www.Jacqueline-Brown.com. If you enjoyed *Out of the Darkness*, please consider sharing your copy with a friend and leaving a review.